# Whatever Happened
# to
# Hansel and Gretel?

## Stories

Introduction by Kim Kovach

Fathom Publishing Company
Anchorage, Alaska USA

ISBN 978-1-954896-26-0 Hardcover

ISBN 978-1-954896-27-7 Paperback

ISBN 978-1-954896-28-4 e-book

Library of Congress Control Number 2023913539

**Credits**

Original Hansel and Gretel story: Jacob Grimm and Wilhelm Grimm (2001 Project Gutenberg). Hansel and Gretel from Grimms' Fairy Tales. Urbana, Illinois: Project Gutenberg. Retrieved June 1, 2023, from https://www.gutenberg.org/ebooks/2591

Cover image: DmitryRukhlenko/DepositPhotos.com

Interior scrolls: olya.erde/Depositphotos.com

fathompublishing.com
Fathom Publishing Company
P.O. Box 200448
Anchorage, Alaska 99520-0448
Printed in the United States of America

# Contents

# Whatever Happened
## to
# Hansel and Gretel?

# Introduction

Kim Kovach

I love writing fiction stories. The experience of creating characters, giving them names, personalities, relationships, and obstacles and then imagining what happens next is pure joy!

After I published my first book of short stories, the local library asked if I would teach a series of fiction writing classes for adults. That was in spring 2007. I have continued to expand my writing classes over the years to more libraries in New York, Connecticut, Massachusetts and New Jersey. Thank you to the librarians for supporting adult writing programs!

Through the wonders of Zoom, my fiction writing classes reach adult participants across the U.S. and around the world with writers living as far away as Colorado, Pennsylvania, California, Alaska, Scotland, Canada, and Quito, Ecuador!

Most adult participants had never written fiction before or at least not since college. We form wonderful, supportive relationships in each writing class. Many of these adult writers are hooked from their first session and continue to write with me year after year. Claire has been writing with me through library writing classes since spring 2011. Angela and Everett proudly keep all of their fiction stories since first joining my writing classes in 2015. Many writers are going on two, three or five years, continuing to sharpen their writing skills as we learn, laugh and write new stories each week.

I have fun choosing topics that inspire creativity and encourage writers to try writing in new genres or from different points of view. Along the way, fiction writers also discover how much fun it is to do a little research to add specific details to their stories. I look forward to each weekly writing challenge because I write the homework stories, too.

In spring 2023, I presented my adult writers with a colorful illustration from an antique edition of the classic Brothers Grimm fairy tale, *Hansel and Gretel*. The original story was published in 1812 by brothers Jacob and Wilhelm Grimm in their first volume of fairy tales. Whatever happened to Hansel and Gretel after escaping from the witch and her house made of candy? The homework was to write a sequel and set the story ten years after the fairy tale ends. What a treat to hear all of the imaginative, descriptive, unexpected stories about Hansel and Gretel in my writing classes that week! Wow!

These stories are too good to keep to ourselves. We are happy to share these creative, surprising and hilarious sequels to the well-known fairy tale of *Hansel and Gretel*. We hope you enjoy reading our stories to answer the question–**Whatever happened to Hansel and Gretel?**

Once Upon a Time . . . .

# Hansel and Gretel

Jacob and Wilhelm Grimm

Hard by a great forest dwelt a poor wood-cutter with his wife and his two children. The boy was called Hansel and the girl Gretel. He had little to bite and to break, and once when great dearth fell on the land, he could no longer procure even daily bread.

Now when he thought over this by night in his bed, and tossed about in his anxiety, he groaned and said to his wife, "What is to become of us? How are we to feed our poor children, when we no longer have anything even for ourselves?"

"I'll tell you what, husband," answered the woman, "early tomorrow morning we will take the children out into the forest to where it is the thickest; there we will light a fire for them, and give each of them one more piece of bread, and then we will go to our work and leave them alone. They will not find the way home again, and we shall be rid of them."

"No, wife," said the man, "I will not do that; how can I bear to leave my children alone in the forest? The wild animals would soon come and tear them to pieces."

"O, you fool!" said she, "then we must all four die of hunger, you may as well plane the planks for our coffins," and she left him no peace until he consented.

"But I feel very sorry for the poor children, all the same," said the man.

The two children had also not been able to sleep for hunger, and had heard what their stepmother had said to their father. Gretel wept bitter tears, and said to Hansel, "Now all is over with us."

"Be quiet, Gretel," said Hansel, "do not distress yourself, I will soon find a way to help us."

And when the old folks had fallen asleep, he got up, put on his little coat, opened the door below, and crept outside. The moon shone brightly, and the white pebbles which lay in front of the house glittered like real silver pennies. Hansel stooped and stuffed the little pocket of his coat with as many as he could get in. Then he went back and said to Gretel, "Be comforted, dear little sister, and sleep in peace, God will not forsake us," and he lay down again in his bed.

When day dawned, but before the sun had risen, the woman came and awoke the two children, saying, "Get up, you sluggards! we are going into the forest to fetch wood." She gave each a little piece of bread, and said, "There is something for your dinner, but do not eat it up before then, for you will get nothing else."

Gretel took the bread under her apron, as Hansel had the pebbles in his pocket. Then they all set out together on the way to the forest. When they had walked a short time, Hansel stood still and peeped back at the house, and did so again and again.

His father said, "Hansel, what are you looking at there and staying behind for? Pay attention, and do not forget how to use your legs."

"Ah, father," said Hansel, "I am looking at my little white cat, which is sitting up on the roof, and wants to say goodbye to me."

The wife said, "Fool, that is not your little cat, that is the morning sun which is shining on the chimneys."

Hansel, however, had not been looking back at the cat, but had been constantly throwing one of the white pebble-stones out of his pocket on the road.

When they had reached the middle of the forest, the father said, "Now, children, pile up some wood, and I will light a fire that you may not be cold."

Hansel and Gretel gathered brushwood together, as high as a little hill.

The brushwood was lighted, and when the flames were burning very high, the woman said, "Now, children, lay yourselves down by the fire and rest, we will go into the forest and cut some wood. When we have done, we will come back and fetch you away."

Hansel and Gretel sat by the fire, and when noon came, each ate a little piece of bread, and as they heard the strokes of the wood axe they believed that their father was near. It was not the axe, however, but a branch which he had fastened to a withered tree which the wind was blowing backwards and forwards. And as they had been sitting such a long time, their eyes closed with fatigue, and they fell fast asleep.

When at last they awoke, it was already dark night. Gretel began to cry and said, "How are we to get out of the forest now?"

But Hansel comforted her and said, "Just wait a little, until the moon has risen, and then we will soon find the way." And when the full moon had risen, Hansel took his little sister by the hand, and followed the pebbles which shone like newly-coined silver pieces, and showed them the way.

They walked the whole night long, and by break of day came once more to their father's house. They knocked at the door, and when the woman opened it and saw that it was Hansel and Gretel, she said, "You naughty children, why have you slept so long in the forest?–We thought you were never coming back at all!"

The father, however, rejoiced, for it had cut him to the heart to leave them behind alone.

Not long afterwards, there was once more great dearth throughout the land, and the children heard their stepmother saying at night to their father, "Everything is eaten again, we have one half loaf left, and that is the end. The children must go, we will take them farther into the wood, so that they will not find their way out again; there is no other means of saving ourselves!"

The man's heart was heavy, and he thought, "It would be better for you to share the last mouthful with your children."

The woman, however, would listen to nothing that he had to say, but scolded and reproached him. He who says

A must say B, likewise, and as he had yielded the first time, he had to do so a second time also.

The children, however, were still awake and had heard the conversation. When the old folks were asleep, Hansel again got up, and wanted to go out and pick up pebbles as he had done before, but the woman had locked the door, and Hansel could not get out. Nevertheless he comforted his little sister, and said, "Do not cry, Gretel, go to sleep quietly, the good God will help us."

Early in the morning came the woman, and took the children out of their beds. Their piece of bread was given to them, but it was still smaller than the time before. On the way into the forest Hansel crumbled his in his pocket, and often stood still and threw a morsel on the ground.

"Hansel, why do you stop and look round?" said the father. "Go on."

"I am looking back at my little pigeon which is sitting on the roof, and wants to say goodbye to me," answered Hansel.

"Fool!" said the woman, "that is not your little pigeon, that is the morning sun that is shining on the chimney."

Hansel, however little by little, threw all the crumbs on the path.

The woman led the children still deeper into the forest, where they had never in their lives been before. Then a great fire was again made, and the stepmother said, "Just sit there, you children, and when you are tired you may sleep a little; we are going into the forest to cut wood, and in the evening when we are done, we will come and fetch you away."

When it was noon, Gretel shared her piece of bread with Hansel, who had scattered his by the way. Then they fell asleep and evening passed, but no one came to the poor children.

They did not awake until it was dark night, and Hansel comforted his little sister and said, "Just wait, Gretel, until the moon rises, and then we shall see the crumbs of bread which I have strewn about, they will show us our way home again."

When the moon came they set out, but they found no crumbs, for the many thousands of birds which fly about in the woods and fields had picked them all up. Hansel said to Gretel, "We shall soon find the way," but they did not find it.

They walked the whole night and all the next day too from morning till evening, but they did not get out of the forest, and were very hungry, for they had nothing to eat but two or three berries, which grew on the ground. And as they were so weary that their legs would carry them no longer, they lay down beneath a tree and fell asleep.

It was now three mornings since they had left their father's house. They began to walk again, but they always came deeper into the forest, and if help did not come soon, they must die of hunger and weariness. When it was mid-day, they saw a beautiful snow-white bird sitting on a bough, which sang so delightfully that they stood still and listened to it. And when its song was over, it spread its wings and flew away before them, and they followed it until they reached a little house, on the roof of which it alighted; and when they approached the little house they saw that it was built of bread and covered with cakes, but that the windows were of clear sugar.

"We will set to work on that," said Hansel, "and have a good meal. I will eat a bit of the roof, and you Gretel, can eat some of the window, it will taste sweet." Hansel reached up above, and broke off a little of the roof to try how it tasted, and Gretel leant against the window and nibbled at the panes.

Then a soft voice cried from the parlour,

> "Nibble, nibble, gnaw,
> Who is nibbling at my little house?"

The children answered,

> "The wind, the wind,
> The heaven-born wind,"

and went on eating without disturbing themselves.

Hansel, who liked the taste of the roof, tore down a great piece of it, and Gretel pushed out the whole of one round windowpane, sat down, and enjoyed herself with it.

Suddenly the door opened, and a woman as old as the hills, who supported herself on crutches, came creeping out. Hansel and Gretel were so terribly frightened that they let fall what they had in their hands.

The old woman, however, nodded her head, and said, "Oh, you dear children, who has brought you here? Do come in, and stay with me. No harm shall happen to you."

She took them both by the hand, and led them into her little house. Then good food was set before them, milk and pancakes, with sugar, apples, and nuts. Afterwards two pretty little beds were covered with clean white linen, and Hansel and Gretel lay down in them, and thought they were in heaven.

The old woman had only pretended to be so kind; she was in reality a wicked witch, who lay in wait for children, and had only built the little house of bread in order to entice them there. When a child fell into her power, she killed it, cooked and ate it, and that was a feast day with her. Witches have red eyes, and cannot see far, but they have a keen scent like the beasts, and are aware when human beings draw near.

When Hansel and Gretel came into her neighbourhood, she laughed with malice, and said mockingly, "I have them, they shall not escape me again!"

Early in the morning before the children were awake, she was already up, and when she saw both of them sleeping and looking so pretty, with their plump and rosy cheeks she muttered to herself, "That will be a dainty mouthful!"

Then she seized Hansel with her shriveled hand, carried him into a little stable, and locked him in behind a grated door. Scream as he might, it would not help him.

Then she went to Gretel, shook her till she awoke, and cried, "Get up, lazy thing, fetch some water, and cook something good for your brother. He is in the stable outside, and is to be made fat. When he is fat, I will eat him."

Gretel began to weep bitterly, but it was all in vain, for she was forced to do what the wicked witch commanded.

And now the best food was cooked for poor Hansel, but Gretel got nothing but crab shells. Every morning the woman crept to the little stable, and cried, "Hansel, stretch out your finger that I may feel if you will soon be fat."

Hansel, however, stretched out a little bone to her, and the old woman, who had dim eyes, could not see it, and thought it was Hansel's finger, and was astonished that there was no way of fattening him. When four weeks had gone by, and Hansel still remained thin, she was seized with impatience and would not wait any longer.

"Now, then, Gretel," she cried to the girl, "stir yourself, and bring some water. Let Hansel be fat or lean, tomorrow I will kill him, and cook him."

Ah, how the poor little sister did lament when she had to fetch the water, and how her tears did flow down her cheeks! "Dear God, do help us," she cried. "If the wild beasts in the forest had but devoured us, we should at any rate have died together."

"Just keep your noise to yourself," said the old woman, "it won't help you at all."

Early in the morning, Gretel had to go out and hang up the cauldron with the water, and light the fire.

"We will bake first," said the old woman. "I have already heated the oven, and kneaded the dough."

She pushed poor Gretel out to the oven, from which flames of fire were already darting.

"Creep in," said the witch, "and see if it is properly heated, so that we can put the bread in." And once Gretel was inside, she intended to shut the oven and let her bake in it, and then she would eat her, too.

But Gretel saw what she had in mind, and said, "I do not know how I am to do it; how do I get in?"

"Silly goose," said the old woman. "The door is big enough; just look, I can get in myself!" and she crept up and thrust her head into the oven.

Then Gretel gave her a push that drove her far into it, and shut the iron door, and fastened the bolt.

Oh! then the witch began to howl quite horribly, but Gretel ran away and the godless witch was miserably burnt to death.

Gretel, however, ran like lightning to Hansel, opened his little stable, and cried, "Hansel, we are saved! The old witch is dead!"

Then Hansel sprang like a bird from its cage when the door is opened. How they did rejoice and embrace each other, and dance about and kiss each other! And as they had no longer any need to fear her, they went into the witch's house, and in every corner there stood chests full of pearls and jewels.

"These are far better than pebbles!" said Hansel, and thrust into his pockets whatever could be got in.

Gretel said, "I, too, will take something home with me," and filled her pinafore full.

"But now we must be off," said Hansel, "that we may get out of the witch's forest."

When they had walked for two hours, they came to a great stretch of water. "We cannot cross," said Hansel, "I see no foot-plank, and no bridge."

"And there is also no ferry," answered Gretel, "but a white duck is swimming there, if I ask her, she will help us over." Then she cried,

> "Little duck, little duck, dost thou see,
> Hansel and Gretel are waiting for thee?
> There's never a plank, or bridge in sight,
> Take us across on thy back so white."

The duck came to them, and Hansel seated himself on its back, and told his sister to sit by him.

"No," replied Gretel, "that will be too heavy for the little duck; she shall take us across, one after the other."

The good little duck did so, and when they were once safely across and had walked for a short time, the forest seemed to be more and more familiar to them, and at length they saw from afar their father's house.

Then they began to run, rushed into the parlour, and threw themselves round their father's neck. The man had not known one happy hour since he had left the children in the forest; the woman, however, was dead.

Gretel emptied her pinafore until pearls and precious stones ran about the room, and Hansel threw one handful after another out of his pocket to add to them.

Then all anxiety was at an end, and they lived together in perfect happiness.

**Jacob** (1785–1863) and **Wilhelm** (1786–1859) **Grimm** grew up in the town of Hanau, Germany. They both attended the University of Marburg where they developed an interest in German folklore. The brothers wrote books about German and Scandinavian mythology and published scholarly papers on linguistics and medieval studies. As academics and university professors, Jacob and Wilhelm Grimm taught Germanic studies. Their lifelong focus became a dedication to collecting and preserving German folk tales which they considered a form of national literature and culture. They set out to collect and document these old tales, passed down in families from generation to generation through the oral traditions of storytelling, before these precious stories were forgotten and lost forever.

The Grimm Brothers' *Children's and Household Tales* was published in 1812 featuring a collection of 86 traditional folk and fairy tales. Many of these early folk and fairy tale stories contained dark themes including violence, horror and child abandonment. Eventually known as *Grimms' Fairy Tales*, the collection was revised and republished many times. By 1857, the collection included more than 200 traditional folk and fairy tales, as well as illustrations. Published in English as *German Popular Tales* in 1823 and more widely available as the *Original Folk and Fairy Tales of the Brothers Grimm*, the English language version contained 156 stories.

Readers owe a debt of gratitude to Jacob and Wilhelm Grimm for having the foresight and determination to collect so many wonderful traditional folk and fairy tales that we all know to this day. People around the world have grown up with the stories about *Little Red Riding Hood, The Frog Prince, Rapunzel, Snow White, Rumpelstiltskin, Sleeping Beauty*, and, of course, *Hansel and Gretel*.

Ten Years Later . . .

# Hansel and Gretel's Cautionary Tale

Angela Blake Fields

Gretel was awakened by the harsh blast of the 5:00 AM whistle which could wake the dead. Sometimes she wished for eternal peace and quiet, which is as good an excuse as any to avoid washing up with freezing water and force feeding herself the stale oatmeal, hopefully with real raisins and not the usual comatose roaches. Just another morning in the Magic Forest Reform School for Girls. She was serving three to five years for the murder of Demona Flickertail, a very wicked witch.

Every reform school inmate has a heartbreaking story and Gretel's was one of the saddest. The sordid tale of Hansel and Gretel includes child abandonment, attempted cannibalism, enslavement and murder. Soon to be a Sight and Sound Theatre Production, something for everyone!

Once upon a time, a family–Father Derwood, Mother Adora, son Hansel and daughter Gretel–barely existed in a small, pitiful shack in the low rent district of the Magic

Forest. The rent was cheap because the neighborhood was overrun with giant trolls. You know the kind–ugly, hairy and smelly with bad attitudes.

Although the family was impoverished, they were grateful for what little they had until the Great Famine, when everything changed. Hansel and Gretel's caring mother, Adora, died of starvation, refusing to cook and eat her children. A wicked stepmother, Evelina, replaced her. Of course she was wicked, is there any other kind?

"Mommie Dearest" convinced the children's clueless father to abandon Hansel and Gretel in the dark, tangled woods because of their ceaseless whining about being hungry. Evelina was not going to starve herself for Derwood's "crumb crushers," Hansel and Gretel.

The father told his children they needed to gather firewood and when Hansel and Gretel weren't looking, he disappeared. Really, looking for firewood when there was a famine, and the cupboard was bare? Luckily the nosey children overheard their parents' abandonment plans and followed the trail of white stones Hansel had dropped earlier. Derwood and Evelina were regrettably surprised to see the children alive and well after they found their way back to the shack.

The siblings were abandoned in the forest a second time after their malicious stepmother successfully convinced their father, the moron, to try again. This time Hansel dropped a trail of breadcrumbs because he didn't have time to gather stones. Of course, greedy birds devoured the breadcrumbs.

The children were tired, lost, hungry, and on the brink of despair, when Gretel spotted a cottage in the forest composed of gingerbread, cake and candy–a dental nightmare. The famished juveniles ran to the house and stuffed their mouths and pockets with delectable treats.

Suddenly, an elderly woman opened the door and invited the children inside for bowls of hot vegetable soup and warm bread. The woman, Demona Flickertail, only pretended to be kind. She was really a wicked witch who built the house to entice hungry children to stop and eat. The gingerbread house scheme was created by Evelina Flickertail, the witch's daughter and surprise, surprise, Hansel and Gretel's stepmother from hell!

After supper, the tired children, who had fallen asleep, were rudely awakened by their hostess who grabbed Hansel and locked him in a cage. Gretel tried to save her brother, but she was knocked unconscious with a heavy broomstick.

Finally, Demona was able to rest after such an exhausting day. She should have purchased the frozen Swanson's Hungry Witch Human Children meals for dinner. She was too exhausted to cook, and Hansel was still scrawny, although she was feeding him around the clock.

The next morning, Gretel was awakened by a loud racket. A mop, bucket, broom, dirty laundry, and garbage were haphazardly arranged nearby while the witch yelled, "Get up and get to work, you lazy cow!"

Gretel knew her rights; child labor laws were supposed to prevent this type of abuse. As soon as she could escape, Gretel was going to report Demona to the Aid for Dependent Children agency.

Hansel was fed breakfast, lunch, and dinner daily because he was being fattened up to be served as the main course at the Magic Forest Witches monthly coven. The members were going to make potions, cast spells, and plan their annual trip to the "Witches R Us Amusement Park" in Transylvania.

Demona checked Hansel's plumpness by pinching his right arm, he would soon be ready. She couldn't wait to try that snooty celebrity chef's recipe for Oven-Braised Young Boys.

Meanwhile, Gretel was exhausted after being forced to complete daily household chores including feeding and walking the witch's pet gargoyle, "Sweetie Pie," a hideous creature with the head of a lion, the body of a goat and the long tail of a snake.

Finally, Hansel was a plump butterball with a popup timer inserted in his thigh. Gretel was not going to let Demona roast and serve her baby brother as the main course. When Demona checked if the oven was 450 degrees by sticking her head in the oven, Gretel pushed her in, locked the door and freed Hansel from his cage.

Oh brother! This kid was a baby hippo, he could barely walk and kept asking for something to eat. Before escaping with Hansel, Gretel checked the oven. All that remained of Demona Flickertail was a mound of greasy ashes, several bones, glass eye, hearing aid, and dentures. As a last act of revenge, Gretel removed the smoke alarm and set the cottage on fire.

Despite Gretel's pleas to the authorities that she killed the witch to save her brother, she was sentenced to three to five years in reform school. While incarcerated, Gretel completed her GED and a BA in Communications. After her release from reform school, she was hired as a motivational speaker for a Fortune 500 company. Last she heard, Hansel was working for Weight Watchers.

The End?

**Angela Blake Fields** was born in the Bronx and currently lives in Greenburgh, New York, with her devoted husband, Everett W. Fields, also a member of Kim Kovach's amazing Creative Writing for Adults which they joined in 2015.

# Sweet Magic

Claudia Wolen

"I don't remember this road being here. Where's the path through the woods?"

"Are you sure this is the right place?"

"This was a narrow dirt path the last time we were here. Now it's paved in cobblestones," said nineteen-year-old Hansel.

"Where are the woods?" asked his younger sister, Gretel. "I recall walking through a dark jungle of trees. We must have our directions mixed up."

The siblings trudged slowly through their memories, trying to decipher the line between then and now.

"Are you sure what happened to us wasn't a dream? How could Papa actually carry out a plan to leave us alone in the forest? How do fathers stop caring for their children? Could we really have been captured by a witch?"

"It was no dream, Gretel. A living nightmare was more like it. I'll never forget how you pushed that nasty creature into the fire and released me from the cage. You saved my life."

"Do you really think we'll find her house after ten years?" asked Gretel.

"I've got to see for myself," said Hansel. "It's the only way my nightmares will stop."

They studied the new cottages that had sprung up along the road.

The smell of freshly baked bread drew their attention towards a small structure with a sign in the front window: *Bäcker*.

"I most certainly didn't buy the breadcrumbs I used to mark our trail from that store."

"If we had passed a store like this, we'd never have ventured deeper into the forest," said Gretel.

Directly across the road was another unfamiliar establishment. In the front window hung long salamis, sausages, and tubes of liverwurst. *Metzgerei* was printed on the sign.

"Had this shop been standing here, the witch wouldn't have found it necessary to eat a live child."

Several horse-drawn carriages clip-clopped by.

"If only our petrifying adventure had taken place ten years later, we'd never have experienced such a horror," whispered Hansel. "Why can't I stop thinking about it after all this time? That frightening night lost in the woods, the candy house, the evil old witch. I was the older brother. I was supposed to be brave and protect you." He sighed. "I should have shown courage. Instead, I ended up sitting in a cage waiting to be eaten. I'm disgusted with myself."

"Stop talking like that, Hansel. The truth is, Papa wanted to lose us in the woods to please that nasty wife of his. He's the one who was a coward."

They passed several more commercial establishments before standing frozen, staring at the haunting sight before them.

Gretel whispered, "I'm positive we've stood on this very spot before. Look at the circles of smoke rising from that tiny stone chimney? It's coming from the fire down below."

"The witch's fire." Hansel only mouthed the words.

"Hansel, you don't think she's still alive, do you? I thought I killed her … but maybe I didn't."

"She couldn't have survived."

"There's only one way to find out for sure whether or not I'm a murderer." Gretel moved forward.

"Please don't … "

Gretel didn't heed the warning. She navigated around several sprawling bushes covered with thorns and tiny red berries. A scrawny black cat streaked across the rutted stone path leading up to the front door. Before she had time to pull back the rusty doorknocker, the wooden door creaked open.

Hansel rushed up to stand beside his sister. Maybe he was a coward before, but he vowed to prove that this was no longer the case.

A tiny woman with a thick braid of white hair stood in the doorway holding a broom twice her size.

"Welcome." Her voice sounded like a tinkling bell. "Come in."

Gretel stammered, "W–w–we were just w–walking by—"

"Nonsense. You've been here before."

Hansel stood up straight and gathered his courage. "We were just on a stroll. This place looked familiar, but we must be mistaken. We'll be on our way."

"No need to rush. Please come in. There's a lot inside that may be of interest to you." The woman stepped back motioning for them to enter.

"Would you like a cup of my herbal tea and a taste of candy?"

"No. We really can't."

"I'm just preparing to open my Magic Candy shop to the public. This used to be the old Gingerbread Cottage until my mother mysteriously disappeared."

Gretel's voice quivered. "I don't mean to be rude, but … was your mother a w–witch?"

The woman's laugh sounded like a jingle bell on a sleigh. "I doubt it, but I don't really know. I grew up living with my grandmother. My mother never even came to visit. By the time she vanished, I was old enough to move here."

They walked along the uneven wood planked floor. In the corner stood an oversized birdcage. In front of them a fire crackled in the stone fireplace.

"We have to go now," the siblings said in unison.

"Don't you want to buy some candy or have your fortunes told?" The woman pointed to a small round table where a crystal ball emitted a pale green light. The walls were lined with glass bowls brimming with candy.

I'm calling my new shop, ***Sweet Magic***." She pointed to a large sign leaning against the wall below the window.

Hansel and Gretel looked at each other. They had been through enough in their young lives to have the ability to read each other's mind.

"We'd like to buy some candy."

"I'd be glad to help you hang the sign outside."

"But, no thank you. There's no need for you to tell us our fortunes."

The End?

When **Claudia Wolen** isn't strumming her guitar in a classroom of young children, she's reading children's books and taking courses to learn how to be a children's book author. Besides kids and music, Claudia loves taking long walks with her dog and thinking up new stories to tell on the way.

# Hansel and Gretel Plus Ten

Richard Mendes

The years have passed since Gretel shoved the witch into her own oven to save Hansel. They have not been easy.

Having been abandoned in the woods twice by their father and stepmother, they were reluctant to go home. Since their breadcrumb trail was long gone, finding their way home was an iffy proposition. They raided the witch's food stocks and set out. After a couple of days, they found themselves at the castle where Cinderella and her new husband, the prince, were living happily ever after. In earlier days, Cinderella had occasionally babysat for Hansel and Gretel's mother and father when they journeyed into town. It took some convincing before the castle's majordomo agreed to mention their arrival to Cinderella.

When Cinderella heard their tale, she cautioned them that the witch had a sister who could be expected to seek revenge once she found out what had happened. Cinderella sent them off to see her fairy godmother for advice.

Cinderella's fairy godmother informed Hansel and Gretel that the gingerbread witch actually had three sisters, the one more wicked than the other. "I feel sorry for you," she said. "Those three play with live ammo, and I'm not about to get in their way. Your best bet is to get on the next boat to the New World. There aren't any decent transoceanic brooms, and they don't have the patience for a sea voyage."

Hansel and Gretel would have taken her advice, but they were penniless. However, they settled on the next best thing and got jobs with a passing circus. Gretel cleaned pots, pans and dishes and washed laundry, while Hansel cleaned up after the animals. During parades and shows, he was armed with a shovel and a bucket to keep things clean for the paying customers.

In due course, one of the evil witches stopped by the gingerbread house and found her sister's ashes. She informed her other sisters, and they set out to find whoever had done in their crisped sister. It wasn't a matter of seeking revenge over the loss of a loved one. Love was completely alien to them. It was simply a matter of if you're going to go into the wicked witch business, you don't want people to get the idea that you could get knocked off. Definitely bad for business!

Wang Pu was the Oriental magician in the circus. He had a droopy black mustache, a wispy black beard, bushy black eyebrows, and long hair twisted into a queue. Herman Frank, the circus owner, promised a leather bag with fifty silver pieces to anyone who could show how

Wang Pu performed his tricks of making things appear, disappear, or turn into birds or rabbits. Nobody ever collected the coins, for the simple reason that Wang Pu was a real magician. Wang Pu's actual name was Josef Kriegmann, and without his costume and makeup, he was bald from the top of his head to his toes. He was also unfriendly, and when not performing, he disappeared into his wagon.

After Hansel and Gretel had been with the circus for a week, Kriegmann pulled them into his wagon one night.

"You are in great danger," he said. "A crow circled us this afternoon, and left a feather in front of your tent. That crow belongs to a witch, and she will be guided here by that feather. Why is a witch after you?"

Hansel told Kriegmann about their adventure in the gingerbread house. Kriegmann nodded. "I thought so. You two are very lucky. I know the witches who are after you. I was their teacher two hundred years ago. They were angry because I would not give them the highest grades, and made up a story that I had molested them. They got the school to fire me, and since then, I have had to earn my living in circuses like this."

Gretel said, "How does that make Hansel and me lucky? You don't seem to have done so well."

"You are lucky because I am a much more powerful magician than they are. And I have long waited for my revenge upon them."

Kriegmann kept his word. Several days later, the three witches descended on the circus at midnight. Kriegmann, in his Wang Pu persona, trapped all three of the witches' spirits and sealed them in Prince Rupert's beads. The beads were surrounded by sand, the sand was sealed in a box lined with lead on the inside and copper on the outside, and concealed in a cave.

"They will be trapped in those beads for a thousand years," Kriegmann told Hansel and Gretel in the morning. "Unless you're still around then, you can consider yourselves safe from them."

Relieved, the two children remained with the circus and their friend. Hansel didn't want to spend the rest of his days cleaning up animals' messes. He studied the circus acts, and came to the conclusion that the crowds were excited by the acrobats, and enjoyed the clowns, though they were less admired. Inspiration came to him, and he and Gretel spent years perfecting an act combining clowning with acrobatics. In due course, they struck out on their own and became famous for their act. Josef Kriegmann gave up the Wang Pu bit and became their agent. He gave them a new stage name, Die Maiers, explaining that the Hansel and Gretel audience was too young for their sophisticated performance.

And they all lived happily ever after.

The End?

**Richard Mendes** has been writing since high school. His first real effort at fiction ended up as a child's book, *Magic in the Stars*, written for his daughter. He published and edited an eighteen-story short story anthology, *Prose & Cons*, after leaving Digital Equipment Corporation, including three stories of his own. Richard spent thirty years in the corporate world, most of it in the field of information technology, and the past thirty years as a computer consultant.
Note: Enjoy a performance by Die Maiers at https://vimeo.com/30014163.

# Gretel's Regret

Kim Kovach

At first, I thought Hansel's idea about eating pieces of the candy house was great. I mean, who doesn't like candy? The peppermint window frames and icing roof tiles were delicious!

After all, we'd been wandering in the dark creepy forest for days, eating nothing but shriveled berries, raw mushrooms and the occasional apple. Hansel had to wrestle a family of squirrels to get their stash of walnuts. That's a sight I hope to never see again!

Anyway, the candy house just appeared out of nowhere. The door handle was made of chocolate, the shutters tasted like peanut brittle and the mail slot was made out of red licorice. With all of that sugar in our bodies, we were so sluggish that we just leaned against a big oak tree and fell into a sugar coma!

Of course, that's when the near-sighted witch showed up. We never expected that! The whole plan of fattening up Hansel and then the old witch ending up in the oven was all over the newspapers after Hansel and I finally escaped. Did you ever smell a witch burning? That acrid smell lingered in my nostrils for weeks.

Well, it was no coincidence that a few years later, my first job offer was from a confectionery shop in downtown Bremen. Oh, it is torture to smell all of that sugar and chocolate every day! Ten hours a day. My step-mother probably had something to do with this cruel idea. I wanted to work in the wool factory using that new invention–a foot-pedaled sewing machine. But no, I have to spend my days dipping toffee and crushing pecans and melting chocolate.

Hansel did not fare much better. Old ladies would literally cross to the other side when they saw Hansel walking down the road. The old biddies would clutch their purses tightly and spit. Of course, father and step-mother chose an awful job for Hansel. He works seven days a week on a logging crew deep in the forest. Not only does Hansel have to wield a giant ax, but he is the one tasked with climbing up the tallest trees to retrieve the unhatched eagle eggs for the King's own aviary. It's very dangerous work.

Our lives are filled with toil and drudgery now. I am more fatigued than a sixteen-year-old girl should be. Sometimes when I am rolling out sheets of taffy or pouring fudge onto the marble slab to cool, I think longingly about that innocent little brother and sister tossing breadcrumbs along the path and then trying to find their way back home through the dark woods.

"Gretel!" yells Franz, the baker. "Stop daydreaming! You'll burn the pfeffernüsse again!"

The End?

**Kim Kovach** is an author, journalist and writing teacher. Kim teaches fiction writing, creative writing and personal story writing for adults and creative writing for teens and children. Kim is the author of the short story collection, *A Few Bad Decisions,* and five books for middle grade readers, including *Welcome to Appletown!, Surviving Vertigo* and the *Kitchawan Kenny* chapter books. Kim writes a weekly newspaper column, Reading, Writing & Chocolate, as well as articles for magazines. Visit her website at www.kimkovachwrites.com.

# A Tale Within A Tale

Martha Paszek

Near the Baltic Sea there once lived a young lad named Hansel, who was a woodsman as had been his father before him. He managed the king's forests. He lived alone in the same hut, where he had been raised as a child, at the edge of a very deep and very dark primeval forest.

One morning, Hansel received a note from the palace. Instead of following the king's bidding, he went to see his sister, Gretel.

Gretel had married the village baker and spent her days behind a counter. As Hansel entered the shop, she stood chatting with customers, exchanging bread for coins. Her blonde braid was tucked under her white cap and her dimpled cheeks were flushed from the heat of the ovens.

"Did you come all this way to buy bread?" asked Gretel.

"No, I came to show you this," replied Hansel taking the letter from his pocket. "It's a royal order to sweep the forest of squatters."

"What will we do?" Gretel panicked.

"I don't know," said Hansel.

As a royal woodsman, Hansel had taken an oath to protect the king's forests. And he did just that, supervising the number of trees removed by the villagers, arresting poachers, and assisting with the king's hunts.

For this work he was given food and lodging, left alone, and asked no questions. All of which totally suited Hansel, because for years he and Gretel had harbored a secret.

Ten years ago, Hansel and Gretel had come stumbling out of the forest with a small fortune in gemstones in their pockets. They had been lost for weeks, their father searching for them.

How to explain those two weeks? Their survival as small children alone in the forest? A fortune in their pockets? Their missing stepmother?

So, Hansel and Gretel wove a fabulous and terrible lie, echoing the ancient tales of Baba Yaga. About an evil witch who ate children and lived in a magical house deep in the forest. About gingerbread and cages and ovens and treasure. About a truly wicked stepmother and some breadcrumbs.

And because it is always easier to accept the idea of witches than to search for the truth, Hansel and Gretel's tale slowly became part of village lore.

Gretel quickly locked the front door of the store and checked the back room ovens. She and Hansel were alone.

"Do we warn her?" whispered Gretel. "She's so far away. Nobody but us knows she's even there."

"It's not only me," said Hansel. "It's all the huntsmen and woodsmen in the entire kingdom. King Ludwig wants a purge. There have been too many highwaymen about not to sweep the forest."

"Then we must warn her."

"If she's still there," said Hansel.

"Of course she's still there. Where else would she go?"

"Gretel, she's had ten years to leave!"

"She's still there," replied Gretel. "It was her only chance for a normal life."

Hansel set out the next day, walking into the deepest, darkest part of the forest. So dark, he had to light a lantern. At night, wolves howled in the distance.

On the third day, Hansel emerged into a small clearing where a little hut stood. Baskets, tools, and wood were stacked near a rough-hewn door. Dried remains of a vegetable garden sat nearby. Smoke, pouring from the mud chimney, announced her presence.

Hansel knocked at the door. He knew she was frightened.

"Rose, it's Hansel. Do you remember me? And my sister Gretel? I have come to warn you."

The door slowly opened, revealing a beautiful, terrified face with long dark hair. The mute girl motioned to Hansel to enter.

"Rose, you have to leave," said Hansel. "King Ludwig's men are coming to purge the forest."

Rose shook her head no.

As his eyes adjusted to the dark, Hansel saw that everything was the same, even the stone hearth where his stepmother had fallen and died. She had struggled with Rose, trying to capture her for a royal bounty. Hansel thought of that wicked woman, lying in her shallow grave, which the three children had dug nearby.

"Rose, please listen," continued Hansel. "These men will take you away. What if they find the grave? What happens when they see your magic? You ran from Ludwig once before."

Rose shook her head no.

"Let me help you." Hansel could see she was becoming agitated.

By now Rose's entire body was shaking. As she opened her mouth to speak, a large ruby popped out, followed by a diamond, and some flowers.

Rose was still cursed.

Rose was one of two sisters who had drawn water from a well for an old woman with magical powers. For her kindness, the old woman gave Rose the gift of gems and flowers every time she spoke. Rose's unkind sister received the gift of toads and snakes.

Unfortunately, Rose's gift backfired. Men pursued her to become rich. She had been running from King Ludwig, when Hansel and Gretel's father found her lost in the forest.

Rose began to sob. An opal fell from her mouth.

As Hansel stared at the gems glittering on the dirt floor, he had an idea. He knew of a family of miners–seven bearded dwarfs who were hardworking and kind. They spent their days digging deep in the mountains searching for treasure.

Long ago the dwarfs had helped another beautiful girl escape from her evil stepmother, the queen. Hansel's father, who as a young woodsman had worked for that queen, had told him her story.

So, Hansel knew the dwarfs would give Rose a safe haven. In return, her magic could provide for them all. The dwarfs had always dealt in gems, so no one would suspect where Rose was hidden.

"Let's pack what you need," said Hansel. "I know a place where you will be safe. We leave here tomorrow."

The End?

Inspired by the fairy tales "Hansel and Gretel," "Baba Yaga," "Diamonds and Toads," and "Snow White."

**Martha Paszek** has always enjoyed writing, both as a student and in her jobs in marketing and non-profits. She recently discovered fiction writing as an empty nester. Martha was born and raised in Falmouth, Massachusetts. She is a graduate of Smith College and now lives in Fair Lawn, New Jersey.

# The Gingerbread Forest

Janet M. Bair

Hansel opened the door to the apartment his sister and her new husband had moved into above the Badenburg Bakery. He breathed in the wonderful scents of dinner and the afternoon's baking.

"Ah, Gretel, there you are. What are you cooking tonight? It smells wonderful in here."

Gretel turned to greet her brother with a hug, while keeping her eyes on the pots bubbling on the stove.

"Potatoes, sausages and sauerkraut. I made plenty. I'm sure you are hungry, as usual. Josef will be home soon and then we can eat."

"We have pumpernickel bread, too," a little voice piped up.

"Two loaves," said a very small girl with brown braids and wearing a worn green dress.

Hansel blinked and looked over at the children. Four children sat quietly on a bench on one side of the table. They watched him with curious eyes.

"Guten tag," said Hansel.

Gretel hurried over. "These are the Ottoschmidt children. They are living with their grandmother now. Meet Fridolin, age ten, Stefan, age eight, Klara, age seven and Johanna, age four.

The oldest child Fridolin said, "Our mother died last week. Father died last year."

Gretel reached over and patted his shoulder. "This is why they have been eating dinner here every night with Josef and me." She smiled up at Hansel, her blue eyes filled with concern and affection.

Hansel smiled back. His younger sister had always had a soft heart and a quick wit to solve other people's problems. Hadn't she been clever to rescue him from the awful witch in the enchanted gingerbread cottage? Even ten years later, Hansel still couldn't stay in a small room with a closed door. He always left all the doors open in his house, sometimes even the ones to the outside. One day a young bear cub had wandered in. He was able to lure it out with a honeycake but he would never tell Gretel about that.

When they first brought the many jewels home from the witch's house, Gretel insisted they move to the city, far away from *any* woods. She had nightmares for years about wandering in the deep woods, lost forever.

The woods didn't bother Hansel, he missed them actually. The woods were a sore topic with Gretel, which is why he had come tonight to talk to her. He looked at the four little orphans again. Not much different from his family now, his father having passed away a year ago. No wonder Gretel felt such sympathy for them. Hunger was a hard thing. The door opened and Josef burst in.

"Guten tag, Hansel, children, Gretel. I hope you will be joining us for dinner?" Josef said.

"Yes, I am looking forward to some of my sister's delicious baking."

"She is a wonderful baker! I'm very lucky to have her as my wife."

"We baked cookies today!" the younger children said.

"You did? Did you save any for me?" asked Josef.

"Yes, my dear. We made ten dozen gingerbread cookies," said Gretel.

"Many animals. Many trees," said Johanna.

"Enough for a whole gingerbread forest!" exclaimed Klara.

Hansel raised his eyebrows. He knew they used to have a tree cookie cutter but Gretel had hidden it away somewhere long ago. The children must have found it in one of the cupboards.

"Well then, I may try each animal," Hansel winked at his sister. "And a few trees."

"Noooo," Stefan and Klara cried. "You would get a tummy ache. We made *so* many different animals."

"In that case, I will just pick three," said Hansel. "Or five. Or seven?"

"Stop!" laughed Gretel. "Don't give them any ideas. Here is your dinner everyone."

She began to serve each one until their plates were full. After they had eaten and they all had at least two cookies (or five or seven–who was counting?), the children left to go across the street to their grandmother's house to sleep. Hansel and Josef helped clear the table and Gretel put a cheerful red apron over her long black skirt to wash the dishes.

Hansel cleared his throat. "I have something to talk about with you, Gretel," he said, pulling at his collar.

"Go on. You can tell me and Josef anything. We have no secrets."

"I have taken a job, a short term one in the Black Forest."

"What?!" Gretel took her hands out of the soapy dishwater and dried them, then sat down at the table across from her brother and Josef.

"You can't be serious," she said.

"I am. It's only for two months. I will be back. Wilhelm is gathering a new supply of wood to carve for the Christmas Market. This year he wants to make new dolls, marionettes, and Nativity sets. He pays well."

"I don't want you to go. What if you get lost like we did? What if there are other witches in the forest?"

"Gretel, we were helpless *children* back then. I carry an ax. Wilhelm will carry an ax and a gun. I don't think anyone will harm us."

"But those woods are dangerous and so far away from our city!"

"That's why we will take the train there and rent horses to travel further."

Gretel stood and paced. "You must *promise* me you will come back at the end of two months. I want to speak with Wilhelm before you leave."

"You shall. I will be fine, dear sister. We will bring back beautiful wood and I will carve a little set of dolls for Johanna for Christmas."

Gretel threw her arms around her brother in a big hug.

"I will miss you dearly. I don't like this but I guess I have no choice in the matter."

Hansel hugged her. "Take good care of her, Josef, and I will see you at summer's end."

After he left, Gretel put the rest of the gingerbread trees into the cookie jar for the children. She bit into a tree cookie absentmindedly, then shook her head. She *really* didn't like forests.

The End?

**Janet M. Bair** is a free-lance writer who has had articles, poetry and devotionals published in over fifty different magazines. She is the author of *Devotions for Young Readers*. A recently retired Children's Librarian, she enjoys reading, sewing, writing and painting. Janet lives with her husband, Jim, in Ansonia, Connecticut. They have two grown daughters and four entertaining grandchildren.

# Beyond the Gingerbread House

Janice Boland

"Quick, Hansel, the witch is baking in the oven, we must leave now," sobbed Gretel, freeing Hansel from his cage.

Racing into the witch's gingerbread house, Hansel called out, "I'm searching the house first. I know the witch hid a treasure in there. And here it is!" he cried, holding up a sack filled with gold and precious jewels.

Hansel grabbed Gretel by the hand. Together they ran through the dark forest, where a great white bird helped them reach their woodcutter father's cottage.

"Mein Gott! Mein Kinder!" cried their delighted father when his returning children burst through the door. "I never thought I would see you again."

When he told the children that their stepmother was dead, they all joined hands and danced with joy.

Then, over a meager supper of thin potato and cabbage soup, they discussed plans for the future.

47

Thanks to the witch's gold and gems, ten years later, Hansel, Gretel and their father were happy and successful.

Hansel, who could never get enough food after his ordeal with the witch, opened a food shop in the Black Forest that sold the finest wursts–bockwurst, bratwurst, liverwurst, as well as sauerkraut, hams, cheeses, breads, and pickles.

Gretel, who had learned housekeeping and culinary skills from the witch, ran a thriving restaurant, famous throughout the Black Forest for serving superb gourmet food–kartoffelpuffer, schnitzels, spaetzles, knödels and, of course, strudels, Black Forest cake, and everyone's favorite cookie–lebkuchen–gingerbread.

On the lower level of Gretel's restaurant was a tavern, a Rathskeller, that rang each night with laughter and merriment.

Dancers in lederhosen shorts stomped and thigh-slapped to the riotous Oom-Pah-Pah music of trombones, tubas, piccolos, glockenspiel, and flutes.

Steins overflowing with foamy beer, brewed by Hansel and Gretel's woodcutter father's nearby Craft Brewery, were raised high in good cheer.

One dark night, a tired, parched, and hungry storyteller, traveling alone through the Black Forest, stopped to quench his thirst at the Rathskeller.

While enjoying a supper of brotsuppe, warm crusty bauernbrot, and Wiener schnitzel, the stranger overheard folks talking about Hansel and Gretel's childhood experience at the witch's gingerbread house.

Furiously scribbling and scribing with his pen, he wrote it all down on paper.

When the cuckoo emerged from the intricately carved cuckoo clock set high on the tavern wall and marked the late hour, Jacob Grimm put down his pen, folded his manuscript, tucked it into his knapsack, and finished his schnitzel.

Then draining the last golden drop of his beer, he left the Rathskeller and continued his journey through the forest. Jacob was most eager to get home and share the tale of Hansel and Gretel and the gingerbread house with his brother, Wilhelm.

The End?

**Janice Boland** is an award-winning children's book author. Her books are enjoyed by children all over the world. She also is an artist, illustrator, etcher, and Haiku poet. Janice was the Editor and Art Director for an educational publisher where she developed and designed books for children and young adults. In addition, Janice taught writing at Western Connecticut State University, Vassar, Manhatanville College and for continuing education programs and libraries in Westchester County. Since 2018, she has been taking Kim's amazing classes at the Pound Ridge Library. Currently, Janice is writing flash fiction, short stories, mysteries and other tales, while portraying horses in oils and capturing images of nature in her Chinese Brush Paintings.

# Hans and Greta

Patricia Humphreys

Greta was preparing the evening meal at the hot stove when Hans tromped into the small apartment. He looked tired after working with the horses all day. Hans took off his woolen cap and jacket and sat heavily on the chair at the table. A thought suddenly occurred to him and he turned to Greta with excitement, "Guess who I saw at the stable today? You will never guess, so I'll tell you."

Greta just rolled her eyes and said, "Alright, who?"

With a sly smile, Hans answered, "Jakob Grimm."

Greta quickly faced Hans, "You must be joking. Was his brother Willie with him? I have never seen either of them, though I wish I could make their life as miserable as they made ours."

Hans made a sour grimace and said, "Isn't that the truth."

Hans thought back to that summer day ten years ago when their father, Franz, had sent them into the Black Forest to hunt for some special mushrooms, the

Pfifferlinge. The best ones were the orange and the yellow. Everyone in the poor little village of Kleinheim was hunting for those mushrooms since people in the cities paid a lot for them. Their father had given them very specific instructions about where to locate the best ones deeper into the forest. Only he knew the location and he told them to keep it a secret. The villagers were too afraid to venture too deeply into the Black Forest. Their father called them superstitious idiots.

Greta and Hans were only eight years old at that time and stayed close to the house most of the time. They lived near the forest on the edge of the village. The villagers were a superstitious lot and believed that Hans and Greta were cursed because they were twins. They thought the twins had caused their own mother's death the previous year. Their father made sure the two of them stayed away from the other villagers as much as possible.

Hans would never forget that day when they went hunting for mushrooms. They left early in the morning and followed their father's directions perfectly. They filled their large baskets with the beautiful mushrooms. Greta brought cheese and bread for their lunch. They had even eaten a couple of mushrooms. He had never tasted any mushroom as good since that day. When Greta took the lead to return to the house Hans argued that she was going the wrong way. After some loud argument, Greta reluctantly followed his direction. It turned out Hans was wrong and they became totally lost.

It was in the early evening, both Hans and Greta were tired and scared, when they saw a light, a campfire in the darkening forest. They rushed toward it, tripping over tree roots as they ran. Suddenly they came into a small clearing. There was a round, beautifully painted wagon, a black and white horse, and a small campfire with a bubbling pot hanging over it. Both Greta and Hans were overcome with hunger and rushed to the campfire. That was when they heard a heavily-accented raspy voice behind them.

"Well, who do we have here? Two beautiful blonde children with such large heavy baskets. Why are you out so late, mein kinder? Are you lost?"

They turned around and saw a very old woman bent over a carved wooden cane as she walked slowly toward them from behind the wagon.

The old woman was dressed in a very long skirt and blouse with a large shawl wrapped around her shoulders and a scarf covering her hair, as all the women in their village did. That was where the similarity ended. To Hans and Greta, it looked like all the colors in the world were contained in her clothing. She was wearing gold earrings, bracelets, and necklaces. They had never seen anyone like her. The women in their poor village only wore drab-colored clothing and did not own any gold jewelry.

The old woman gestured to them, "Sit down, sit down, already. You look very hungry. I will give you some food." When she reached them, she looked down into their baskets filled with the large golden mushrooms, "Ach, mein Gott, what beautiful Pfifferlinge. Do you think we can throw some into the pot for dinner?"

The twins nodded silently at her and then sat on the ground and waited for the food.

The old woman went back to the wagon and came back with metal plates and a water bag. She served the meal to the children. Just as she was about to serve herself, she said, "I forgot to add something." Taking a small vial out of her skirt pocket she poured some of it into her hand and sprinkled it over their food saying, "Here you go, mix that in, it'll make it taste better," and put the vial back into her pocket.

Hans and Greta ate ravenously. The old woman laughed merrily at them, her numerous wrinkles making her eyes disappear. After they finished their meal, they looked at the strange painted wagon. Both children petted the horse on its forehead. The horse was also different from the villagers' draft horses. It was a little smaller with a long white mane and tail. Even its hoofs were covered with fine white hair.

Both started to yawn and could not stop. Their eyes drooped heavily. The old woman laughed, "It is time for you two to sleep. You have had a very hard day. Here, I have put blankets around the fire and you can sleep there tonight. I will show you the way home tomorrow morning."

They nodded their heads sleepily, said goodnight and collapsed down on the blankets.

The next morning, their father Franz found them sleeping on the ground near the cold campfire with two empty baskets near them. When they woke up, they told him about the old lady and how she had helped them. "You scared me half to death when you didn't come home yesterday," he yelled. Then looking at the empty baskets, "Where are the Pfifferlinge? Did that old gypsy take them? Such bad luck," he shook his head. Looking at them, he laughed, "That'll teach you to trust strangers."

In the evening, Franz left the twins sleeping and went to the village tavern. As he drank his beer, he told the story of his children and the old gypsy woman. The next day the whole village was talking about it and the story slowly began to change. There was again talk about the cursed twins.

The following week, old farmer Sigmund, who was a great storyteller, took his fruits, vegetables, and mushrooms to the market in the nearby big town. There he told the story of Hans and Greta to a group of local towns people. As the story circulated around the town it changed again. Now the gypsy had morphed into a witch and the wagon into a magical house. The Grimm brothers, passing through the town, heard the story at the hostelry where they were staying and were very impressed. The brothers decided to tinker with it to make it more horrifying. They knew that everyone loved a good horror story.

The Grimm brothers published their book of fairy tales nine months later and it included the tale of Hansel and Gretel. Old Sigmund learned about it at the market in the big town and came back to the village. He said the story in the Grimms' book was the real story and that Franz had lied. The villagers got scared and angry. They said the twins were cursed. Fear spread like wildfire and the villagers said the witch was going to come and get their children. The villagers decided that Franz and his children should be run out of the village. A friend of Franz ran to the house and told Franz he and his children had to leave immediately. The villagers might hurt him and his children. That very day they left Kleinheim, carrying their possessions with them. Later they heard that a group of angry villagers had burned their house to the ground.

Hans sat at the table thinking about all of the hardship his family had gone through before they finally settled in Vienna. The move turned out to be a good thing for both Hans and his father. Franz found work as a carpenter and Hans worked with the great Lipizzaner stallions. The Grimm brothers should really pay for the harm they did to his family.

As Hans and Greta sat at the table eating dinner, they talked of ways to get revenge on Jakob Grimm. Finally, Greta said, "Why don't we just put a special gift in his traveling coach. Something he will never forget."

Since they were twins, Hans knew immediately what Greta meant and laughed uproariously.

Both laughed so hard they fell on the floor and that is where their father Franz found them when he came through the door. He stared at them, "What is the matter with you two, get off the floor. Are you crazy?" He just shook his head and said, "Greta, I want my dinner. Now!"

Early the next morning, Jakob Grimm was leaving the hostelry in a hurry. His coach was brought out front. He opened the coach door, quickly stepped in and sat down in something moist and squishy. A horrible smell rose and flies surrounded him. Jakob then saw a piece of paper that said, "A gift from Hansel and Gretel." He erupted from the carriage cursing and screaming. There was a big brown stain on the back of his pants.

Meanwhile, in a nearby alley, Hans and Greta watched excitedly and laughed like loons.

The End?

**Patricia Humphreys** is a retired librarian living in Pennsylvania's corn belt. She enjoys reading mysteries and science fiction, pursuing nature photography, watercolor painting, and long walks in nature. Writing is a new venture for Patricia, but she hopes it will be a long lasting one.

# Gretel's Revenge

Lisa Acerbo

"Today's the day," Hansel said.

"Maybe." Gretel frowned at her reflection in the mirror, noticing a crease on her brow. "But not likely." At eighteen, she was much too young for wrinkles. Unfortunately, the experience at the witch's house was forever etched in her mind and apparently on her face.

"You must choose." The reproach in his gaze stung. "No more stalling." Hansel took Trudy's hand. They'd been married three years and ever since the ceremony, Gretel's relationship with her older brother had dissolved much like the gum drops on the crone's cottage.

"Are you excited?" her father asked.

"As thrilled as yesterday, and the day before that, and the day before that, Papa." Gretel rose to leave the dining room. "I must ready myself."

Trudy scoffed.

Running to her quarters, Gretel sank into the plush window seat and shed a single tear. Just as quickly, she wiped it away, refusing to let anyone witness her distress. Not that anyone ever entered her room except the servants. Her brother and his wife didn't care, father wouldn't dream of intruding on her personal space, strange men would be improper, and female acquaintances were few and far between.

A sour laugh skittled out of her mouth.

Taking down the witch had brought her family fame and glory, especially her brother. Selling off the contents of the old crone's magical candy cottage commanded more money than they could ever use. Turning the cottage into a museum provided her father with the goodwill of the townspeople.

Gretel, on the other hand, received only the oh-so-lovely nickname Crone Killer and another cage. First poverty, then the witch, now this. In her palatial confinement no one planned to roast her for dinner, but this prison still had bars. Her father, as oblivious and malleable as ever, wanted her happiness through a good marriage, but her brother and his wife wanted her gone, and they were getting rather mean about it.

After donning a shimmering gold day dress, she coiled her sun kissed blonde hair into a long braid that fell to mid back. Her mind drifted and Gretel realized the family apple didn't fall far from the tree. As soon as word went around that Hansel held some rather large purse strings, the women flocked, and her brother, like Papa, picked the worst of the bunch, a money-hungry gold digger that wanted Gretel and Papa out of the picture. The couple couldn't wait to marry her off and send her packing, father in tow.

A knock on the door roused her from her thought.

"The line grows long today," a young servant said. "Are you ready?"

"Let's get this over with." She clutched the long skirt in one hand so it would not sweep the ground, seized a book in the other, and headed to meet her suitors.

The line of men snaked outside the front door, down the garden path, and around the corner of the mansion. Two hundred or more future husbands, all waiting to speak with her. They lined up for many reasons: money, fame, challenge, but did any of them line up to find love?

She searched for a good heart and kind soul. Appraising the line of men, some in armor, others carrying gifts, Gretel needed to rely upon her wits once again. Hansel's claim to fame had been using the breadcrumbs to find their way home, but that had been her idea.

The worn, leather-bound book, the witch's grimoire, warmed her hand. Gretel had pilfered it from the candy cottage and spent her nights memorizing spells. Now, the words to seek true love flew from her lips.

When she'd first spoken the incantation, Gretel had been surprised how few men had the capability for devotion. Of the possibilities, she'd rooted out those more than twice her age or so hideous she'd shuddered at the thought of seeing them undressed. One suitor had come close, but his habit of eating garlic and onions with each meal was too much to stomach.

All day, Gretel dismissed prospective fiancés with the wave of her hand. At the end of the line, a tall, gangly young man, sweeter than chocolate kisses, waited to meet her.

"What's your name?" Gretel asked. "You really do shine bright."

"Jeffrey."

"You're not afraid of me, the Crone Killer?"

"I love strong, beautiful women."

"Let's walk and talk then."

Jeffrey and Gretel went for a stroll, and she learned a most important fact. The next day, they were betrothed.

"When will we meet this man?" asked Hansel a week later.

"He's coming for dinner tonight." Gretel was at the dining room table, helping the servants lay the place settings.

"Lovely." Trudy's smile was triumphant. "We'll finally get to enjoy this house once you marry and move. Unfortunately, your dowry is less than expected. There's always lots of work needed on the property. Gardens don't grow themselves."

At that moment, her betrothed walked in the door. Gretel ran over and linked her hand with his. "Trudy, I think you know Jeffrey."

"My brother!" Trudy screeched. "You want to marry my brother?"

"Yes, let's keep it all in the family. Since he's the eldest, we'll stay in the house and let you find another."

Gretel conjured a gum drop from thin air and placed it on the table as the centerpiece. "For good luck." Her gaze settled on her family to see if anyone dared contradict her.

"Jeffrey, you cannot mean to kick your sister out of her house."

"Whatever my soon-to-be wife wants, she gets."

And with that, Hansel was once again on the road, but this time without Gretel's smarts and with a witch permanently in tow.

The End?

**Lisa Acerbo** is Program Chair at a local college. She lives in Connecticut with her husband, three dogs and two cats. When not reading or writing, she enjoys drinking exorbitant amounts of coffee, hiking, and attempting to convince her husband they need another pet.

# ZauberDorf

Claire Quinn

Schwartzwald, Baden – Wurttemberg, Germany

*Tales around Town*–This is Prince Charming reporting to you from ZauberDorf, our Enchanted Village. Whether you ride a broom, climb a beanstalk, cast spells, or stir a cauldron, we have all spilled from the pages of our fairy tales. We embrace our beauty and goodness and malevolence, all at once. Denizens of a bewitching world, we've settled in the planned community of ZauberDorf, a gated, self-governing enclave for senior fairies with reasonable HOA fees. You won't find ZauberDorf on any particular latitude or longitude and your GPS won't help you, dear. It exists in southwestern Germany with Strasbourg, France near the Vosges Mountains to the west and Switzerland to the south. ZauberDorf lies in the heart of the Black Forest or as locals call it "Schwartzwald." Schwartzwald is where the controversial story of Hansel and Gretel took place and where the fall out continues a decade later.

ZauberDorf sits in the depths of this famously dense forest, far below the weak filtered sunlight, under carpets of moss, protected by all manner of woodland creatures, mostly unknown to the secular world.

But this magical spot is of its time and citizens are willing to rethink past decisions. The crime alleged to have been committed by Hansel and Gretel has become a lightning rod for controversy. The family members of the deceased witch, Rosina Leckermaul, have their respective supporters as do Hansel and Gretel who are supported by ZauberDorf law-and-order groups. The opposing factions have coalesced into two groups, polarizing the town. Those seeking to wave their own banners for unrelated fringe causes such as fracking and climate change in the Black Forest have joined the fray and civil unrest is threatened.

This is all taking place against the backdrop of a dozen cold cases of missing children within a mile of Rosina Leckermaul's cottage dating back to a decade before her murder. Coincidence?

What at first seemed a clear-cut heroic tale is now viewed through the lens of distrust and suspicion. Parental abandonment and subsequent escape and self-defense from a predatory, cannibalistic witch is now purported to be murder and grand theft with ancillary charges pending. Unsurprisingly, pressing for a trial are the family of the witch and the witch community in ZauberDorf. ZauberDorf law-and-order groups want all charges against Hansel and Gretel dismissed immediately.

Hansel and Gretel have been charged with **Theft** for binging on their father and stepmother, Brunhilda's, food supply; **Littering** for leaving pebbles and breadcrumbs in the woods; **Destruction of Property** for happening upon a gingerbread house which they promptly began to eat. The young siblings were welcomed into the house by its elderly occupant, the deceased Rosina Leckermaul, who provided them with soft beds and plenty of food while ministering to their needs and fattening them up. They were also charged with **Murder** because Gretel pushed the witch into her own oven thereby killing her and for **Felony Burglary** for stealing the witch's gems and precious stones after the assault. The siblings then returned to their father, whose wife, Brunhilda, had conveniently died under suspicious circumstances and all continued to live on the dead witch's wealth.

There is a litany of lesser charges such as impeding a police investigation and obstruction of justice pending, as well. Their father is accused of being an accessory after the fact. The witches have formed a class action suit and are suing Hansel and Gretel for defamation of character. Should this case move to trial, seven jurors are usually needed. The dwarfs function as town jurors since they are mostly impartial and know all the gossip.

A fundraiser for Hansel and Gretel is being held on the green with Peter Pan and Wendy Darling hosting. Featured acts are Pinocchio and Geppetto, Glinda, the Good Witch, Snow White, Cinderella and Tinker Bell.

Staging a rally with the Witch Community and led by the Red Queen will be the Wicked Fairy, Wolf W. Wolf, the Evil Queen, the Wicked Witch of the West, and the Evil Stepmother.

Ali Baba and his forty thieves will rob all of their houses while they are out.

As is customary, after the trial, the headless horseman will ride his white steed through ZauberDorf and read the verdict for all to hear.

The End?

**Claire Quinn** has enjoyed writing fiction since she was an avid eight-year-old reader in New York City. After a thirty-year career in Financial Services, Claire and her family moved to Pound Ridge, New York, and she was able to focus on the world of words and writing. Claire has been writing with Kim and her gifted students for the past twelve years and hopes for twelve more. Now that would be a real fairy tale.

# The Further Adventures of Hansel and Gretel

Everett W. Fields

It's been ten years since my encounter with the witch. Now I can't believe I've been summoned to appear before the council for suspicion of murder. It is well known that my sister Gretel and I did away with the wicked witch, but it was truly a matter of self-defense—*she was going to frickin cook and eat me*. Gretel was the one who pushed her into the oven, something she never lets me forget. She also blames me for leaving a trail of bread crumbs to help us find the way back home.

"How could you be so stupid; you should have known birds would eat bread!" she scolded.

Well, that's all I had, when father told me we were going out to pick berries. I knew it was a ruse, they gave us only stale bread to take with us. She had no complaints when I marked the way home with the stones when father tried this before.

Gretel and I have been estranged for quite a few years now. She was the one who pushed the witch into the oven. I was never given any credit, now I was being blamed for the whole thing.

Then there was the situation with father. He married that evil woman, he never stood up for us, he brought home food for the family, but she hid it from us. And Gretel had the nerve to take his side.

He should have been arrested for child abuse or at least neglect, but Gretel didn't see it that way. She said that stepmother had him under her influence and he didn't know what he was doing. I think he knew damn well what he was doing, and I also questioned his story that our mother abandoned us. I think he drove her away. I feel he may have even killed her, but I have no proof.

Gretel became a celebrity; all the papers ran stories about how this brave young girl stood up to a terrible witch and saved herself and her brother from being devoured. She met a prince in Copenhagen and they were married. She now lives there in a castle. Father threw me out of his house because of my accusations. I found my way back to the gingerbread house and lived there for a while. The gingerbread began to mold, and the mold has affected my breathing, so I can't hold a job. When I appealed to Gretel, she wasn't completely heartless, she agreed to send me 100 marks a month on the condition I never bother her again. I agreed to it, what other choice did I have?

A new sentiment has taken over the country and the government has been persuaded to investigate the many killings of witches. Witch hunts had been common in

Europe and are continuing to this day. Certain groups are calling for reform. They allege that 35,000 people had been put to death, many of them falsely accused because witchcraft is used to explain the occurrence of random misfortunes such as sickness or death, and the witch provides an image of evil. So, after ten years, they are casting doubt on our story. I say story because Gretel cooperated with Jacob and Wilhelm Grimm in writing their book of fairy tales. Gretel's connection to the prince seems to have protected her from prosecution.

So, they came after me, saying I plotted to take this lady's home after she was good enough to take us in when we got lost in the woods? They believed father's story that we had become separated because we wandered from the crooked tree where he told us to wait. I knew he purposely abandoned us, but no one would believe me!

At the hearing, I told my story to the magistrate. I explained that we slept outside in the *Long-Lost Woods,* and we were cold and hungry, trying to find our way home when we came upon the gingerbread house. The witch was very nice at first but once we were inside, she trapped us and fattened me up, clearly stating her intention to eat me.

"Did you not tear off pieces of her house?" asked the magistrate.

"We were only nibbling at the gingerbread because I used the stale breadcrumbs to mark the path, so we had eaten very little."

"How would you like it if someone showed up at your home and began tearing it apart?"

"We were very hungry, sir. I'm afraid we acted out of desperation," I explained.

"So, if your story is true, you and your sister killed this woman because you feared she was going to eat you. Why then were there pearls and precious stones missing from her house? How am I not to believe that you two murdered her and stole her property?"

"I know of no stolen items."

"Perhaps your sister took them."

"Then why did you not summon her here as well?"

"Because she resides in Denmark. Unfortunately, this office has no jurisdiction there. I have gathered all of the facts; I will consult with the other commissioners, and I will issue my decision. Please wait out here."

After what seemed like hours, the magistrate returned.

"Mister Hansel, after much discussion, we have concluded that we do not have enough evidence to hold you responsible for the death of Miss Haig or the theft of her jewels. However, if we find further information, you may be called in once more. You may go!"

So, there were missing jewels. Anyone could have stolen them after we left. Or did Gretel go back and take them? I always had doubts about her story of meeting the prince and moving so far away.

The End?

**Everett W. Fields** was born in White Plains, New York. He's lived in nearby Greenburgh most of his life except for a short stay in The Bronx, home of his wonderful bride, Angela. He graduated from Elmhurst College in 1973 and spent 37 years working as a customer service representative and central office technician for Verizon Communications. After he retired, Angela convinced him to try his hand at writing. After writing with other groups in the Westchester Library System, he found a home at the Bedford Library and Pound Ridge Library writing with the wonderful participants in the groups led by Kim Kovach.

However . . . .

# Hansel and Gretel
# A Journey to Freedom

Virginia Bulzacchelli

It's been more than ten years since the pair outsmarted the wicked witch and escaped into the forest. It took weeks to find their way back home. No bread crumbs to follow this time ... their stepmother feigned relief at their survival though secretly she was angry that her plan had failed.

Memories of the horrific experience continue to haunt them to this day. Gretel's nightmares are vivid and as real as when they were held captive by the witch who fed them cookies, cakes and sweets to fatten them up. Gretel remembers peeling off bits of gingerbread from the doorframe hoping to find a way out.

When she was caught by the wicked witch she'd say, "It is so delicious I just couldn't resist taking a bite." She has never again eaten gingerbread since that fateful day.

Being back at home did not relieve their stress. They felt as though they were being watched. Once Hansel became so ill, he was convinced he had been given poison venison.

On a tip from their evil stepmother, Hansel was arrested and charged with willfully pushing the gingerbread cottage witch into the oven. He was plunged into jail to await trial.

His attorney, Alibi Dashawish, instructed him not to talk about the case. "You are innocent until proven guilty."

The court date was set for six weeks from Thursday. Hansel was to plead 'not guilty.'

Gretel, being much younger, was exonerated due to her involuntary contribution to the actual crime.

The prosecutor, Henry Rigged, was adamant: Hansel was guilty! The prosecutor believed he had the proof. He tried a bribe, "If you confess, I promise you will receive a lighter sentence and be eligible for parole within six months."

It didn't work. Day after day, Hansel was questioned, and day after day he refused to confess. "I'm not guilty. It was self-defense."

"Ah, so, you admit to pushing Witch Hazel into the oven?"

"I'm not guilty, it was self-defense," he repeated day after day.

The prosecutor, determined to get a confession, brought in Gretel for questioning. She, too, refused to confess to a crime.

On the day of the jury trial, the twelve jurors chosen from a select group of countrymen, all swearing to be impartial, sat riveted to their seats as Mr. Rigged questioned Gretel.

The courtroom filled with their peers. Jurors were sympathetic and showed actual horror when Gretel said, "I'm glad Witch Hazel is dead. She can never hurt anyone ever again. She was wicked."

"Why do you say that?" asked Mr. Rigged continuing to question her.

"She would place me in a cauldron over the fire until it got so hot, I would cry out."

"And how many times did she do that?" he asked.

"Almost every day … Just a little game she would say … until the day she lit a big fire in the oven. She bound my hands and feet … she put me in the cauldron and brought the heat of the water up until I couldn't stand it. When I cried out, she stuck an apple in my mouth and sprigs of rosemary in my hair."

An audible gasp came from the courtroom with everyone whispering and wiping their eyes.

Pounding the gavel, Judge Handpicked cried out, "Order in the court."

"Then what happened Miss Gretel? You're still here," asked Mr. Rigged sarcastically.

Crying now, Gretel said, "She was opening the oven door to put me in when Hansel broke free from his restraints and ran toward her. He gave a mighty push to get her away from me and she fell into the oven and he slammed the door shut."

"So, you say your brother pushed Witch Hazel into the oven?"

"Objection!" cried Alibi Dashawish, Hansel's lawyer.

"Sustained!" said Judge Handpicked pounding the gavel.

"No further questions," said Mr. Rigged reluctantly. "You may step down."

With all witnesses questioned and last arguments presented, Judge Handpicked sequestered the jurors to the jury room to carefully consider all of the evidence and come back with their verdict.

The jury was given bottles of water and locked in the room with instructions to elect a foreman, debate the evidence and ring the bell when a verdict was reached. Small pads and pencils were placed on the table in front of every chair.

Carefully considering all of the evidence and reviewing all of the testimony, the jurors reached a verdict in less than an hour. The foreperson notified the bailiff that a decision had been reached. The bailiff then notified Judge Handpicked.

Returning to the courtroom, the court clerk asked the foreperson, "Have you reached a verdict?"

"Yes, sir, we have," she replied.

The court clerk ordered Hansel to stand and handed the paper to Judge Handpicked.

"How do you find the defendant?" asked Judge Handpicked.

"We find the defendant Not Guilty," said the foreperson.

Judge Handpicked pounded the gavel and said, "You have been acquitted. You are free to go."

The courtroom erupted in cheers and hugs while Hansel and Gretel's evil stepmother quietly left the room.

Hansel and Gretel, now free to uncover witches, gathered an army of crime stoppers to hunt them down.

"They are so normal," says Gretel. "They hide in plain sight."

The End?

**Virginia Bulzacchelli** joined Kim's fiction writing class in 2018 after reading a description of the class on the Pound Ridge Library's website. Virginia has been retired for thirteen years and at eighty-one years of age is still an avid gardener. She enjoys the weekly Zoom writing classes and homework assignments. She is inspired to be more imaginative and continues to venture on. Virginia lives in Pound Ridge, New York.

# Ever After

Kelly Gavin Guerra

Every year on the anniversary of the siblings' miraculous homecoming, Gretel performed a penance. Unbeknownst to anyone, especially to Hansel, she would rise before the sun and delicately dance a series of complicated steps to avoid the floor's creaks and groans. *"Left, left, right, right,"* she sang to herself, *"then straight ahead and out of sight!"* Since the woods, she had keenly honed her sense of direction.

Once outside, Gretel would fall to her knees beneath her bedroom window, which stared into the mouth of the forest. Solemnly, she would turn the familiar soil by hand, unwilling to risk the clanging of a spade against stone. She would dig until her fingernails grazed the cool metal links. Instantaneously, she would feel a surge, intense and electrifying, throughout her body. It wasn't until she bowed her head and secured the chain around her neck, though, that she would feel the power dripping from her pores. This was where her contrition truly began.

Gretel would bear the cross around her neck from sunup until sundown. In these hours, her soul darkened. She became mean, tortured, chaotic. And then, of course, there was the magic. Suddenly, Gretel was able to move things just by looking at them. She could produce food or jewels from thin air. Though enchanting, this power came with a price. Always, Gretel found herself drawn most to those she loved, ready to inflict unimaginable pain. Perhaps in a subconscious attempt at protection, Gretel would eventually isolate herself, taking to solitary confinement in the one place no one would look for her: at the grave of her stepmother.

* * *

Gretel never truly understood what had happened to the witch who had married her father. Somehow, while she and her brother were being prepared for slaughter, the woman had disappeared. "She is no longer with us," her father explained, tears trickling down his weathered face. Days after their return, Father erected a headstone without a burial plot–there was no body with which to fill it. He placed the marker reverently at the edge of their property, overlooking the lake. It read, *Gone, but not forgotten.*

Today marked Gretel's tenth act of atonement. She trudged to the now overgrown gravesite, golden pendant thudding against her heart with every step. The boys, knowing the date and too uncomfortable to engage with an emotional member of the fairer sex, left her be. They assumed, as they always had, that Gretel was simply mourning the only mother that she had ever known.

*How lucky they are*, she murmured to the dewy grass, *so blissfully unaware.*

Gretel, you see, was not blanketed with grief for Mommy dearest who had abandoned the children to die in the woods; good riddance to her. No, it was guilt that weighed poor Gretel down–guilt for the life she herself had taken that day ten years ago.

She braced herself as she approached the headstone, suffering already constricting around her heart. She anticipated hours in the unforgiving sun, its heat so like that of the wretched oven. She awaited the hatred that would clog her veins, the impulses she would need to reign in. Never, though, did she expect to see another figure already bowed in penitence: her father.

"Darling girl," he sighed as she approached, draping his arm around her bony shoulders. "I couldn't bear to leave you out here, all alone, again. I share in your sadness. Though this day brought us riches and your glorious return, it also brought heartbreak. You need not suffer alone."

He turned toward his daughter and leaned in to offer a bear hug. When his eyes caught a glimpse of the shining metal chain around her neck though, he pulled back, gasping. "My dear, where did you find that necklace?"

For a singular moment, Gretel contemplated revealing the truth. How much lighter would she feel after setting her guilt free? Would divulging that she was a murderer allow her to reclaim some of her lost innocence? Would she be able to look herself in the mirror?

Her confession was on the tip of her tongue when her father continued, his pallor that of a ghost: "That belonged to your stepmother. I ... I haven't seen it since she was taken from us."

Gretel's vision instantaneously blurred and she imagined the Earth beneath her was swallowing her whole. She closed her eyes, steadying herself, and flashed back to the day that changed her young life forever. She saw herself, beckoning the witch closer to the oven, feigning ignorance of its machinery.

Her hands itched as she recalled the scratchy wool of the old woman's overcoat, and her breath hitched when she replayed that final shove of their captor into the flames. She could almost taste the adrenaline that led her to Hansel's cage, and then to rob the witch of her treasures.

She remembered her fingers clutching the necklace, then pocketing it quietly, away from the rest of their riches. She reflected on the willpower it took to run from the body she burned to ash without looking back.

"Gretel," her father gently nudged, "did you take that from your stepmother?"

"Yes, Papa," Gretel professed, the most she would ever say on the matter for the rest of her life.

"I see, and you've been coming out here year after year, to remember her," he presumed, nodding in understanding. "Sweet child, we must accept that she is gone, unable to return despite our greatest wishes. Here," he reached out his hand, "let us say goodbye."

Together, Gretel and Papa dug a small, square hole, directly in front of the headstone. Together, they buried the necklace alongside their guilt and their grief.

And then, together with Hansel, they lived happily ever after.

The End?

**Kelly Gavin Guerra** is an avid reader and a budding writer. She graduated from Boston University and now lives in Connecticut with her husband and spoiled cat. She hopes that this publication will show all of her students that they CAN achieve their dreams!

# Ten Years After

John-Paul Marciano

Ten years after their encounter with the witch, Hansel and Gretel were now in their late teens. Hansel, now a woodcutter like his father, was a strapping young man with broad shoulders, thick muscular arms and legs, shoulder-length blond hair with bangs, and expressive blue eyes. Gretel was a comely young lady with wavy waist-length strawberry blonde hair she liked to keep in a braid when she was cooking and cleaning. While Gretel had the same expressive blues eyes as her brother, that was where the similarities ended.

Gretel was about twenty-five centimeters shorter than Hansel and about eight stone lighter. And while Gretel spoke in soft, gentle tones, Hansel had a husky, gruff voice. After their father died of pneumonia three years earlier, Hansel took over the role of household provider while Gretel assumed the household duties. Unlike his father, Hansel was proficient with a bow and arrow. With his skill, Hansel was able to provide wild boar and deer meat to sustain his sister and himself with enough left over to barter for goods with the village tradesmen.

Wanting to do something other than housework, Gretel traded some venison for a bow from a bowyer in a neighboring village and a quiver of arrows from a fletcher in the same village. Initially, neither craftsman was willing to make the bow and arrows for her. But she lied and told them they were a present for Hansel.

Determined to help Hansel, Gretel hastened through her daily chores so she could spend an hour each day practicing with her new bow and arrows. After several weeks of practicing, Gretel's confidence grew. She decided it was time to test her skills. She set out into the woods to look for small game. It didn't take her long to bag three rabbits and a squirrel. After bringing her catch home, she prepped them to be cured. While Gretel was preparing the evening meal, Hansel came home and noticed the rabbit and squirrel meat stretched and hanging by a window.

"What is this?" Hansel queried pointing to Gretel's catch.

"Some rabbit and squirrel meat," Gretel replied with a bit of pride.

"Hmm," Hansel said. "What did you trade for it?"

"Nothing," Gretel replied. "I shot them myself."

Hansel furrowed his brow. "How is that even possible?" he asked in puzzlement.

Gretel's face lit up as she smiled knowing her brother was confused. "I've been practicing."

Hansel, still confused, shook his head. "Practicing? With what? I don't understand."

Gretel, still amused by Hansel's befuddlement, walked over to the cupboard where she kept her bow and quiver of arrows.

"With these," Gretel said handing Hansel the set.

Hansel laid the quiver on the kitchen table and inspected the bow. He raised the bow as if to shoot an arrow and pulled on the bowstring.

"This is a nice bow," Hansel said still playing with the bowstring. "Where did you get it?" he asked.

"I went to the bowyer in the village south of here. I traded him for some of the venison we had," Gretel replied. "I thought we had more than enough to spare and I didn't want it to go to waste."

Hansel had placed the bow on the table next to the quiver and was now inspecting one of the arrows.

"I got the quiver of arrows from the fletcher in the same village for some boar meat," Gretel said.

Hansel was now rolling the arrow on the table. "The fletcher does nice work," he said as if in a trance. "The arrows are true, good craftsmanship. Better to hit what you're aiming at." Hansel looked up and made eye contact with his sister. "And he just made them for you?"

Gretel held her brother's gaze. "I had to lie and tell him they were a present for you. He wouldn't have made them for me. Said he doesn't make arrows for lassies."

Hansel smiled. "That sounds like something Bagh would say. You should have him make you a set with steel arrowheads."

"I was thinking silver," Gretel said.

"That's awfully expensive to shoot deer or boar. Don't you think?"

"But not too expensive to slay witches," Gretel said.

Hansel laughed. "What witches are you planning on slaying? There haven't been any witches around here since you locked that witch in the oven years ago."

"I'm not so sure," Gretel said. "I went for a walk in those woods about a month ago. I didn't have much to do that day so I decided to go by that witch's house. Someone is living there."

The smile on his face changed to a look of concern. "Are you sure?"

"Yes, I'm sure. There was smoke billowing from the chimney," Gretel answered. "At first, I thought I was imagining things. But I watched the house from inside the woods. Eventually a woman came out and sniffed the air like a dog that caught a scent on a breeze. Initially, I thought it was the witch from years ago. But when she came closer, I noticed she looked similar. Maybe she's related."

Hansel's eyes narrowed as he mulled over what Gretel told him. After a few seconds he said, "Have two quivers of arrows made with silver arrowheads. If Bagh won't do it, I'm sure I can get Johann to make them. But Bagh makes better arrows than Johann."

"I can tell when you're plotting something," Gretel said. "What's going on in that thick skull of yours?"

"I'll check the place out while you're having Bagh make those arrows. Get some holy water too," Hansel said. "If she's a witch we should eliminate her. We can team up."

"What's the holy water for?" Gretel asked.

"We'll dip the arrowheads in the holy water just to be on the safe side."

Gretel nodded.

"Oh, and Gretel."

"Yes?"

"When you shoot small game, aim for the eyes so you don't waste any of the meat."

Gretel gave Hansel a curious stare as he left to wash up.

The End?

**John-Paul Marciano** graduated from the University of Notre Dame with a B.S. in Mathematics. After teaching high school mathematics for a year, he moved into IT. Starting out as a software engineer, he held several positions including systems analyst specializing in performance measurement and capacity planning. Now retired, he devotes much of his free time to creative writing. In 2019, John-Paul's short story "Torn" placed third in the Connecticut Press Club Communications Contest. He is also a content contributor to Wikipedia, having written the article "Battle of Soissons (1918)" and has supplied numerous additions and corrections to several articles.

Possibly . . .

# Hansel and Gretel, Ten Years After

Martha Jankovic

Hansel and Gretel began running rapidly away from the fire-breathing dragon, along with the rest of the villagers, as quickly as their feet could carry them. It had been ten years since they had last faced such imminent danger. Hansel and Gretel had been taken hostage by a witch who lived in the forest, after their dad had abandoned them in the woods on their stepmother's orders. Hansel had been held in a cage to be fattened up for a meal for the witch, and Gretel had been forced to do her bidding. They had escaped when good fortune had enabled Gretel to push the witch into her own oven to bake. She then released her brother from his cage and the two siblings had fled the house. They had returned to live with their father. Their stepmother had passed while they were held captive the forest. Now their dear father has recently died.

Suddenly, Gretel tripped and fell down. Hansel stopped to help her, of course, but the other villagers ran away faster and left them behind. The two young adults froze and looked straight into the face of the dragon, who also stopped in front of them, taking in the situation. The dragon pointed with his small forward hand toward Hansel's canteen which hung around his neck on a cord. Following his instinct, Hansel tossed the canteen to the dragon. Awkwardly, the dragon opened the canteen and took a swig of water, and then another. He cleared his throat and then began to speak.

"Hansel? Gretel?" asked the dragon in a very deep voice.

The siblings looked at the dragon in awe, and Hansel practically whispered, "Yes?"

After Hansel helped Gretel to her feet, with her sore knee seeming to be the least of their current problems, the dragon went on to tell them his tale.

"I remember hearing your voices upstairs when you were at the witch's cabin in the woods. She had locked me in a cage in her basement, after stealing me away from and killing my mother. I think that she wanted me as a pet and was fattening you up, Hansel, to feed to me and herself. She must have enchanted me to enable me to speak. While I am grateful for that, I have been cursed to constantly breathe out fire, which always scares away potential listeners, until I have a sip of water first. As you might imagine, it's been a difficult time for me, since no one else would talk to me, and they always run at the first sign of fire. Some have tried to kill me, and frankly I've been so sad lately that I almost allowed it. But something inside me told me that I must keep going, in the name of my mother.

"I'd hoped that I would one day find you both to thank you for ridding us of the evil witch. I managed to break out of my cage, strongly motivated by the smell of fire, which might have been my mother's spirit in me, in addition to the smell from the oven upstairs.

"Since I am mostly reptile, I think I survived after the witch's demise on little sustenance until I got the hang of outdoor forest living, which included eating and enjoying the awesome vegetables from the witch's magic garden. The garden flourished after she was gone. Something tasted particularly good and I grew very large. I've learned to not eat too much of it or I keep getting frighteningly bigger. After all of these years, I think that I must be adult size, just like you two, and I am very happy to meet you. I am afraid that the rest of the villagers are not as kind and understanding as you and likely won't allow me to stay or visit here often. But I am full of joy to finally meet you."

Hansel and Gretel looked at each other, with wide eyes, and then Gretel asked the dragon, "Well, you have certainly been through a lot. What is your name?"

The dragon took another sip of water and answered, "I'm not sure who named me, but I've always felt like a Sylvester, and I would be honored if you would call me that, too."

"We would be honored to do so," replied Gretel. At that point, Hansel, Gretel, and Sylvester walked off into the forest to the witch's old house, which Sylvester had made into his home, next to the magical garden and a full, flowing river. The three new friends spent a lovely afternoon together discussing the past and present and future. They did not see the spirits of their ancestors shining upon them, praising peace, but they likely felt them. Sylvester had become quite a good chef and prepared an excellent meal from the garden vegetables which they all enjoyed.

When evening approached, Hansel and Gretel told Sylvester that they would try to educate the villagers not to fear him and promised to return to visit often.

They did, spending many wonderful times together and enjoying all of the adventures which time would allow. Sometimes they even roasted marshmallows.

The End?

**Martha Jankovic** has always enjoyed writing, from the documents and various communications which she has written during her career as an attorney, to her weekly fiction writing classes with Kim Kovach via Zoom which she began several years ago. When not writing, Martha enjoys ice and inline figure skating, gardening, reading, cooking, and spending time with her family and friends.

# Hansel and Gretel

Carmella Cammarota

The witch is dead. Hansel filled the pockets of his lederhosen with all of the witch's gold. Though it was heavy, he could carry it because he'd been well fed by the witch in anticipation of her meal. Gretel, who had survived on bread and water, was thin and weak. Her rosy cheeks gone, she determined to find strength enough to push the witch into the oven. She wore some of the witch's jewels around her neck and ears, on her clothing, rings on her fingers, and carried some in the pocket of her red apron. They crammed precious stones in between the food they took in a basket which they carried together. A large swan miraculously appeared and conveyed them across the lake and into the forest they recognized as home.

Father was overjoyed to have his family together. The wicked second wife he had unwisely chosen had choked to death greedily eating a huge piece of their goat that she had killed. Gone was their supply of milk, but they were rich now and could live well. Gretel cleaned the hovel that had once been their charming little cottage and cooked meals to fortify her family. They bought a cow, a goat and chickens. They planted a garden and cleared out old thin trees to create an orchard that would supply food, jam and beverages for themselves. But there was a problem.

Hansel was losing weight and strength because he was having nightmares of the witch wanting to eat him and his body could not tolerate smelling or eating chicken or meat. Gretel cooked all the food he could tolerate with the finest olive oil, herbs and seasonings and brown flaky powder from the huge earthenware jug Father had hidden from the wicked stepmother. They did not know what this powder was, but remembered that when Mother was alive, she mixed it into the flour of the bread she baked, dropped spoonfuls into the delicious gravy of the stews she cooked, and breaded strips of chicken with it before roasting.

No one in the family had been sick when Mother was alive. Fevers, grippes, sickness that would at times overtake their village never made them sick. When she sensed illness, she concocted a hot drink of honey and the juice of vegetables or fruits, always adding a spoonful of the brown powder. Mother had not revealed the secret of the magic brown powder. Gretel wondered and worried about it, but decided it was worth a try for Hansel and in a short time he began to regain strength. His nightmares stopped and he was able to start a venture to help poor villagers.

He purchased a property on the main road and erected a building with facilities to store food during all seasons of the year. His friends helped by advertising and raising funds from store owners and others who could afford donations to feed and start schooling for poor families. The gardens and orchards at Father's house provided more than they needed. Fruits and vegetables were brought to the town where they were given for free until the poor were able to contribute a bit so others could benefit.

By then, Hansel could not resist the delicious smells of cooking meat that surrounded him at home. Gradually he overcame his total disgust of meat ... but the question remained. What is the brown powder that kept his family well? It remained a secret.

The years passed quickly and the family grew. The cottage had been enlarged into a comfortable house. Gretel and her husband lived there. Hansel would surely find the girl of his dreams soon and begin a family as well. He was busy now with his old friend, Kurt, who had studied medicine and was the town's doctor. They were determined to improve living conditions for their town as well as elsewhere. When not providing care for patients, Kurt was consumed with research.

Hansel saw an opportunity to satisfy the mystery of what was in the jug. He brought some of it to Kurt, telling him only that it was found in their cottage and asked him to use his knowledge, skill and equipment to determine what it was. Kurt was delighted with the task and began eagerly. He placed a mound of the brown powder on the sterile white examining table and smoothed it out. There were small dry stubby bits, larger soft smooth pieces, fragments with dried veins, needle-thin straight pieces that broke when touched, a bit of dark green moss and many tiny specks of all colors, dark and light brown, black, green, tinges of yellow and orange, barely noticeable in the mix. There was no strong odor, just that of a powder kept airless in a container.

Time passed, but they remained clueless despite Kurt's knowledge and his precision microscopes. He would not give up. Hansel and Gretel were worried that the magic powder would be used up before yielding its secret to good health. They worked diligently on their gardens and orchard, and enjoyed the results, but were annoyed by the creatures that ate their plants and fruits. They screened off what they could from the rabbits, deer and birds, but there was no stopping the insects which ruined their crops. They installed sticks in the garden with strips of wet tar to trap some of them and brought them to Kurt asking for a solution to the problem.

Kurt enjoyed examining the insects. Most of them, even those that appeared ugly to the naked eye, were beautiful under the microscope. Their shapes and colors varied to fit into the landscape and the plants they were after. Kurt saw browns, blacks, blues. Something struck him as familiar, very familiar. Had he seen things like this before? Where? Is it possible, he wondered? Who would believe this and might be willing to test the theory he was developing?

He would. Kurt began his own project of trapping insects, spiders, grasshoppers, crickets, bees, earthworms, but no flies or any that carry disease. He prepared them to die naturally and dried them, and after weeks he crushed them. There was a resemblance to the brown powder. What did that mean? His study of nutrients and which ones were needed to maintain good health and develop strength brought him again to the need for protein as an essential element. He subjected himself to the test and began each day with a small amount of his dried insects spread on buttered bread or stirred into his coffee. They did not taste as good as cinnamon and sugar, but they caused him no harm. After a month, he felt stronger and less fatigued than before. When he was sure he had found the answer to the strange brown powder he presented his findings to Hansel. After more research and experimentation, they decided to produce quantities and present them for sale. A small packet would be enough for a family for a month.

It was not expensive, but there were not many takers. Little did they know that in the world were countries that had been consuming insects in varied ways for thousands of years. Now we, hundreds of years after Hansel and Kurt's discovery, are on the path of the thousands before us. How did Hansel and Gretel's mother know about this when people in Europe did not? Was she somehow tuned into a different part of the world? Then and now many of us reject the thought of insects as food. However, consuming insects as a means of improving health may be a good reason to accept this difficult challenge.

The End?

**Carmella Cammarota**, during her thirty-year career as a K-12 school librarian in Westchester County, New York, enjoyed traveling, reading and writing of all kinds. Kim's weekly writing classes have given her the opportunity to continue writing and listening to the short stories written by talented writers in the classes.

# Hansel and Gretel, Redux

Debbie Gilbert

Hansel and Gretel anxiously arrived at the docks on the west side of Manhattan, where the steamship would deliver their beloved father, Hermann, to them. They had arrived three years earlier on that very ship, paid for with money their father had kept aside to give his children a better life. It was the 1860s and there were no decent jobs in Germany, so their father sent them to the land of opportunity and promised he would follow once they got settled.

When they first arrived, they lived with their aunt, who had moved to America ten years earlier. Hansel worked as a carpenter and had a steady stream of work as the city continued to build housing for the influx of immigrants. He saved as much money as he could after contributing to the household for his upkeep. Gretel became a live-in nanny to a widowed gentleman living near Central Park, a beautiful oasis recently built for the enjoyment of the city's residents.

Her employer was a wealthy financier and a gentleman named Sampson Tuttle. He tried to spend as much time as he could with his two young children, which endeared him to Gretel. Over two years, Gretel's love for the children deepened as she cared for them like her own.

One day, in the park, the children, their father and Gretel found themselves behaving every bit the normal family. Samson and Gretel sat on the picnic blanket as the children frolicked with other children. Samson looked at Gretel with affection and asked her if she would consider becoming his wife. This was unexpected and Gretel found herself dumbstruck. She looked down at her hands, which were tightly woven together. Samson patiently waited for her to absorb this news, which he knew would be a shock to her. He had never before shown overt interest in her as a partner. She stammered, mostly from the surprise of it all, though she did have feelings for the man. He told her to take her time considering his question. She knew she would be happy with him and adored his children, so she unfurled her hands and let him take hers into his and said she would be honored to be his wife.

Gretel was excited to soon introduce her intended to her father. She had written to her father about Samson but not about their engagement. They held off setting a wedding date until he arrived. She could not imagine not having her father give her away. She knew the two men would get on famously, Samson being very much like her father in temperament.

The ship's loud horn made Gretel jump. She and Hansel looked at each other with anticipation and smiled. As the ship got closer to the dock, they looked up and could see their father waving to catch their attention. Gretel could feel goosebumps rise on her arms. Hansel could not stop smiling. They missed their dear father so much. Their parting was very hard on all three of them as they were so close before their departure. Now they would start a new life in America, together.

The reunion was splendid. They held each other for what seemed like forever. After having a picnic lunch prepared by their aunt, they set out to her home to complete the reunion of Hermann and his sister, Else. Hansel was doing well financially and took a place of his own in Murray Hill. Hermann took Hansel's place in his sister's home until he settled in and found employment.

After the family spent time reacquainting themselves and filling in the details of the past three years, it was time for Gretel to tell her father about her engagement to Samson and the children. He listened intently, his facial expressions alternating between smiles and concern. Gretel could not tell whether or not he was happy about her upcoming marriage. But she felt confident that once they met, her father would come to love Samson as much as she did. She thought that his reservations might be because of the children, but they too would become endeared to her father, she was sure. Samson and his children had already become treasured by Else, which is how she was so certain.

They all were invited to Samson's home for dinner. He was careful not to be too formal since he knew Gretel's family was from a modest background. After dinner, Samson and Hermann went for a walk. Samson professed his love for and devotion to Gretel and assured him he would take good care of his daughter. Hermann asked whether they were planning to have more children. He wanted a grandchild of his own blood. Samson said he would be guided by what Gretel wanted, but assured Samson that he would consider his children to be Hermann's grandchildren, should it be his wish.

A wedding was planned and took place in New York's Astor Hotel the following year. It was a modest affair by standards of Manhattan's financiers. Hansel was best man as he had become close to Samson. One year later, Benedict Hermann Tuttle was born. Hermann moved into the cottage on the Tuttle property so he could be near the family. He came to treat his adopted grandchildren as his own and was very happy.

Hansel met Sadie Hanson six months after his sister's wedding. They married a year later and moved close to Hermann, Gretel and Samson and their family. Two years later Sadie delivered Hildy and added to the family's legacy and joy.

And they all lived happily ever after.

The End?

**Debbie Gilbert** has been writing since junior high school. In her business career, she did a lot of writing, so when she turned to fiction, she had to change the paradigm, adding words instead of cutting them. Ms. Gilbert is also a visual artist, favoring textiles, sculpture and photography. She is retired from a wide variety of occupations and loves to learn, volunteer, and travel. Ms. Gilbert has two adult sons and lives with her husband in Trumbull, Connecticut.

# All That Glitters

Constance Taylor

The old woodcutter lived alone in the forest after losing his wife when a large tree cracked and fell in an unexpected direction. He feared his skills were lost and grew afraid to walk in the woods. He believed his two children had died when famine had walked the land and he had abandoned them in the woods. The man had not known one happy day since he had left the children in the forest.

He lived in sadness and with great remorse until the day his children returned.

Hansel and Gretel rushed into the small cottage and threw their arms around their father.

"How is it that you have returned to me?" the old man asked.

The children recounted their story of finding the gingerbread house and meeting the witch. Then Gretel emptied her pinafore until pearls and precious stones were scattered about the room. Hansel threw one handful after another out of his pockets. The children joined hands with their father and they danced together among the gems.

Later, the children and their father gathered up the pearls and precious stones, wrapped them in an old apron, and buried them at the base of the tree beside the house.

"These trinkets will only bring despair to those who trade with them," their father explained. "Good does not come from evil sources."

Years passed. The famine that had burdened the land lifted. A time of plenty came allowing the country to heal from the strains of the time of great hunger.

Healing was hard to find in the home of Hansel and Gretel. Johann, their father, grieved sorrowfully for his part in abandoning his children. His name meant "God is gracious" in German. He told his children over and over how sad he was that he had not lived up to the name his parents had bestowed upon him. Johann struggled daily to make amends to the children.

Gretel became a homemaker for her father and brother. She kept the house clean and prepared daily meals. Her tender care deepened Johann's wounds. On many nights, he lay awake cursing himself for accepting his daughter's help when he had once turned her out into the forest.

Hansel and Johann worked together and Hansel became an accomplished woodcutter. Where Johann had cut and hauled wood only to be burned, Hansel kept the finest sections of the trees from the fire. He carefully stored and dried these sections. When winter came and the days were short and dark, he carved wonderful creatures. First, animals of the forest: deer, elk and bear. As his talent grew, he also carved the smaller animals: rabbits, otters and beavers. News of Hansel's skill spread throughout Germany. Soon a trail was beaten through the forest to the woodcutter's cabin by folks wishing to purchase the wonderfully carved animals.

Years passed by as if in minutes. Hansel and Gretel watched their father age and grow weaker. One day, Johann was too weak to go to the forest with Hansel. He took to his bed. Not many more months had gone by before Johann passed to the next life.

Once Johann was no longer present to monitor his children's lives, Gretel spoke with Hansel of her dreams. "Now that Father is no longer with us, I wish to live in the city and wear fancy dresses. I am tired of being nothing more than a handmaid in a poor cabin."

"But how can one woodcutter earn enough to keep you as you wish to live in the city?" Hansel asked.

"We must dig up the old witch's jewels. That will make possible the life I wish to lead."

Hansel argued for many days but Gretel would hear none of his words. She demanded that Hansel help gather the jewels for her.

Finally, Hansel agreed saying, "Sister, I am tired of your constant barrage of words. I will get the jewels and then you must leave and never return."

And so, Hansel dug beneath the tree. He dug deeper and then wider but did not find the jewels.

Gretel came out of the house. "What is taking so long?"

Hansel spoke, "Something has happened to the jewels. I have dug this deep hole and still found nothing. Perhaps I have accidentally shoveled them out."

"Let us look though the pile of dirt carefully then," said Gretel.

Brother and sister carefully sifted through the dirt and set aside scraps of cloth and bits of metal.

"Look closely," Hansel said. "This is the apron we wrapped the jewels in and these bits are the chains and fasteners in which the jewels were set."

They sat side by side on the dirt as their eyes opened to the truth. The jewels had been nothing but sugar molded into diamond shapes. The pearls only white icing formed into tiny balls. The sweets had melted away with the winter rains leaving behind only the scraps of cloth and bits of metal.

The End?

**Constance Taylor** left California to become a commercial fisherman in Alaska in the 1960s. She fished salmon, crab and shrimp for twenty years in Prince William Sound. She then settled in Cordova to become a printer and art gallery owner. Constance moved to Anchorage in the 1990s to work as a paralegal, auctioneer, and bookkeeping consultant. Now she's a photographer, publisher and author. Her children's books include *Midnight on the Alaska Highway* and *Growing up in Alaska: A Baby Arctic Tern,* and *Sik-Sik: An Arctic Ground Squirrel Tale.* Visit her website at www.fathompublishing.com.

# Hansel and Gretel: The Aftermath

Jennie Scalisi

Although there was blight upon the land, Hansel and his sister Gretel found themselves instead in good circumstance. It was ten years ago when Hansel had filled his pockets with colorful stones and seeds for planting as they escaped from the witch's candy house. They also carried some bread and cheese stuffed in a sack to sustain them as they searched for the path back home. When they had finally arrived, their father was no more than skin and bones. He was sad and lonely after the death of his wife from typhus but was overjoyed when he saw his children once again.

With the father's help, Hansel planted the seeds he had taken and whimsically added to the dirt one smooth emerald stone for good luck in a would-be garden of hopes and dreams. He buried a sapphire gem just a stone's throw away and a ruby one several meters further. When the family depleted the little food that Hansel and Gretel had gathered in their haste to flee, there was nothing else left to eat. The candy house had long since disintegrated into dust and ash soon after the old witch was roasted to a crisp in the belly of her wood burning stove.

The family set out on foot in search of food in nearby towns, walking for days on end. But it soon became apparent that other villages had also succumbed to the great famine. Despite their exhaustive travels they could find not even a few potatoes or head of cabbage. They turned back saddened and empty handed. The father agonized over what to do and prayed for a miracle. They were weak and disheartened but when they caught site of their tiny home, they stared in amazement. What they found was that the seeds they'd sown before leaving had taken root and now a lush garden full of greens was revealed.

There were giant heads of lettuce, cabbage and rows of big leafy spinach. Vines of green beans and carrot fronds peaked through the fertile ground. A few meters away rosy apples hung from multiple limbs in an orchard where there were also peach trees that brimmed with their succulent fruit.

After eating their fill, they ambled about the grounds and came upon a small stream which had helped to irrigate the garden and orchard. As they drank from the clear crystal water, the father scratched his head in wonderment of it all. In the area where Hansel had planted the red stone, sturdy maple and oak trees now stood. This would provide them with much needed firewood using the flint found by the stream. Over time, the father and Hansel grew strong and they felled trees to build a shed. Here Gretel stored the fruits and vegetables diligently preserved and canned for the winter.

Word spread that this family had food and soon strangers from all around arrived daily. Hansel and Gretel's father offered what he could and, in return, many bartered their services to maintain the productive garden or build additional shelter. A growing cooperative developed and erected even more homes and eventually a school house, a church and even an orphanage. It was not uncommon for many children to have been abandoned by their families in their attempts to survive; now a refuge was provided for the homeless children. Hansel's father had found a way to atone for his past sins when he had reluctantly abandoned his own children.

As the legend unfolds, there came to pass a young orphan girl named Ingrid. She was of the same age as Gretel and both grew up in the village where they played and attended school together. When Ingrid was older, she was smitten by a young man who was passing through on his travels and she left the village to be with him. In time, Hansel took a wife who bore him three children. And Gretel was betrothed to a strong handsome lad she met in church. It was a time of peace and harmony within the community.

One day, the king and his knights happened upon this self-sufficient village. He discovered, to his chagrin, that no taxes had ever been paid to the kingdom. Angered, the king accused the father of underhanded dealings, mischief and evil magic as the reasons for the town's prosperity. The king ordered that the father be arrested and taken to the castle where he would remain locked in a cold damp dungeon for a very long time. By happenstance, a young maiden would pass his cell each morning on her way to gather water for her horses. Hansel's father was very thirsty but his thirst was more for conversation than water. One day, he called out to the lass to ask her name. He meant no disrespect he said; he just hoped to hear another person's voice. She said her name was Ingrid and she hoped to wed the prince once the king granted his approval.

She could not tarry long for fear that she would be admonished for speaking with a prisoner. Yet every few days she went to check on this gentle elderly man who asked for nothing but a kind ear. She learned that he had been taken from the very same village where she had grown up and been cared for in the orphanage after she was abandoned by her family. From the next few visits, Ingrid gleaned that this man was actually Gretel's father; the very man who was responsible for saving her life. She immediately sought out the prince in an attempt to spare this man's life.

The prince went to visit Hansel's father and questioned him thoroughly to determine the truth behind the transpired events. He wanted to know how the family came into such good fortune while the rest of the land suffered. Although he found the story hard to believe, the prince appreciated the benefits of these so called 'miracle seeds and magic stones' and was grateful for the family's benevolence. He released the father immediately and a joyous feast was held in his honor. The king gave his blessing to his son's upcoming marriage to Ingrid and promised to support the philanthropic endeavors of the Hansel and Gretel family farm and village forever.

The End?

**Jennie Scalisi** is a retired emergency medicine physician who discovered a new passion for writing. She enjoys exploring this creativity in Kim Kovach's Writer's Inspiration classes since 2021. In addition to writing, Jennie now finds time to pursue other activities including reading, book clubs/author talks, bicycling, nature hikes, gardening, and baking sourdough bread.

# Hans and Greta – The "Lebensfreude"

Shari Kay Mokhtari

A bellow of laughter came from the round table of five laid with the finest white linens and china and adorned with delicacies galore. Greta wasn't sure why she had bought this grand home, but was always thankful when she could fill it with those dearest to her.

"Oh, my gosh, Greta, that is hilarious," said Emma.

"Did she actually think you were flirting with her best friend's husband?" asked Hans.

Greta continued with her story. "Yes, and all I did was lean over the table and introduce myself to the unknown gentleman. That's when Ana snidely remarked, 'He has a wife and she is very pretty.' Then she started giving me the death stare."

"Wait, did you have on that dress with the low neck?" asked Freida.

"Well, … " said Greta blushing. "I may have, but that is no indication of my intentions. I was simply introducing myself to the strange man that everyone else at the table seemed to know."

"Ana can be such a *hundin*," Franz said putting his arm around Freida. The table burst out laughing again.

"That's a horrible thing to say, Franz, we are all going to hell for laughing," Freida scolded.

It wasn't that Freida actually cared but she felt she had to be the sensible one of the lot. Franz and Freida had been together as long as Hans and Greta had been famous. Franz was the one who helped them tell their story and have it published by the Brothers Grimm. The siblings knew he was a true friend to be trusted.

Greta gave a bittersweet smile at this act of affection by Franz towards Freida. It was uncommon for a German man to be so tender. She hoped one day to be able to find that kind of love. For now, Greta had only her brains, sense of humor and quick wit. It was, after all, those things which kept her and Hans alive so many years ago. Surely there was a man who would also appreciate those things and not just want her for her fame and fortune.

Hans stood up, clinking his silver spoon on his custom-made crystal wine glass. "Attention, attention please. I would like to toast my lovely bride to be on her twentieth birthday," Hans said holding up his chalice. "My dear Emma. I knew the moment I ran into you at *der bonbon laden*, fate had brought me to you. I hadn't been able to step foot in a candy store since my childhood, but on this day, something was calling me, to see if my fear had passed. I am sure you thought it odd to see a grown man standing at the door, timid to step over the threshold into a rainbow world of candy. But instead of judging me, you were so kind, and brought different sweets for me to try at the door without me ever having to come inside. Even after the shop closed, you continued to bring them to me one by one. Not once did your kindness waiver, not once did you shoo me away. Thank you, my love, for your unconditional support. Happy Birthday," he finished and kissed her on the cheek.

"*Ein Prost,*" followed Franz raising his glass. "To Emma." They all cheered as their crystal glasses clinked together.

Greta looked around again. Her best friend, Franz, happily married; Hans, her brother, her everything, nearly married. She was so happy for them both, truly she was, yet deep down she felt alone. It was like a weed embedded in the pit of her stomach and slowly it started weaving its way into each organ, squeezing them one by one until it invaded her heart.

Hans saw the hidden look of quietness on his sister's face and quickly clinked his glass again. "I have yet another toast, or more of a proposal, for my sister," he said reaching his hand towards Greta. "Franz and I have an idea and we need your help."

Franz quickly stood up, recognizing what Hans was about to ask. "Well, it is just an idea in the works, Greta, nothing final yet," he interrupted nervously.

"Oh, poppycock, it is going to work and, with Greta on our team, this is going to be huge, a game changer. Greta, we need your brains. Franz and I have come up with a new invention," Hans said with giddiness. "It is called the *Luftpumpe.*"

"The *luftpumpe*?" Greta asked, "What does it do?"

Hans began to explain, "It is a small bellow, similar to one you use to blow air on a fire. However, this one has a tube attached so you can push air into other things, such as a bicycle tire. It is brilliant," said Hans complimenting himself.

"It is brilliant," Franz chimed in.

"And what do you need me for?" asked Greta.

"Well," Hans paused to take a sip of wine, "to create it and make it work, of course. We are only the inventors. You, Greta, you are the thinker and the creator."

Franz added, "We will also be the sellers. Hans and I have already been working on a catchy saying. Shall we, Hans, show the ladies what we have?"

Greta, shaking her head, thought to herself: this is so typical of these two. Figure out how to sell something that doesn't fully exist yet. An air pump for a bicycle of all things!

Hans and Franz were now standing side by side with their backs to the table, ready for their performance.

Franz, trying to imitate a squeaky voice, said, "What do you do when your bike tire goes poo?"

Hans' equally bad voice followed, "How do you fare when your tire is out of air?"

In unison, they said, "Who do you call if your tire has taken a fall?"

They both then jumped and turned around facing the girls.

"I'm Hans," said Hans.

"I'm Franz," said Franz.

In unison, grinning broadly and flexing their arm muscles, they both shouted, "And we are here to pump your tires up!"

The three women burst out laughing. Emma had just taken a sip of wine and, unable to contain her laughter, she sprayed red wine all over the table and fine linens.

"It's a good idea, yes?" said Hans to his sister.

"Yes, Hans, it is a good idea. I will be happy to help," replied Greta, leaning back in her chair and observing her surroundings. The feeling of aloneness had been calmed by thankfulness. Thankful for her friends, for her brother, and for herself. She knew her time for love would come, but she had so many other things to accomplish first.

The End?

**Shari Kay Mokhtari** has a secret love of writing stemming back to high school. Her craft includes writing poetry, children's stories, and adult fiction. In her extra time, she enjoys spending time with family, gardening, reading, and, of course, letting her imagination go wild with writing.

# The Final Ingredient

Jessica L. Hughes

It haunts me in the night.

The sugary walls dripping syrup … marshmallow stones and chocolate bricks forming the foundation of the house … the ever-present scent of burning caramel but never knowing where it was coming from … the excess of candy and peppermint and vanilla all perfuming the air at once. The memories burning into my mind's nose.

But even worse is the reminder of the oven, the smell of an ever-burning fire, her wretched shrieks as I pushed her and let her cook and turn to charcoal and ash like …

I can't even think about it like this. I did something unforgivable. Something that I should be publicly punished for, even if I did have no other choice.

My brother doesn't feel that way. "You're my hero," he says reassuringly to me when the dark thoughts begin to flood my mind and my focus diminishes. "You did what you had to do, Gretel. It was me or her."

But why did I have to make such an ungodly choice at all? I was only eight years old, a little girl enslaved by a wicked woman who had kept Hansel locked in a rusty cage like an animal. We had already been abandoned by our penniless parents. Betrayed by birds who sang lovely songs but who also greedily consumed the breadcrumb trail Hansel had dropped to help us find our way home. I had already suffered an ill fate.

And yet, God found it necessary to hand me over to a woman who would train me to prepare my own brother for a dinnertime spread.

The wicked woman, owner of the tempting, colorful, sugar-drenched abode, taught me her recipes: her thick, fragrant soups and hearty stews, decadent roasts and savory casseroles. She taught me how to cut vegetables and use spices. She taught me how to cook meat that I never knew the origin of … I just knew it was there, stored somewhere in the house. She taught me these useful skills, skills I should have learned from my mother, just for the sole purpose of devouring Hansel when she deemed him plump and rich enough for her liking.

And now, those rich, delicious recipes stir inside my head like potatoes, turnips and carrots, unfinished and begging for their final ingredient.

I had to do it.

Hansel and I are older now. I am eighteen and I help my mother in the kitchen, preparing pies and other delights to sell to the villagers. Hansel works in the fields with Papa, bringing back wheelbarrows of wheat and fruit for us to turn into decadent desserts.

We never truly forgave our parents for leading us away and abandoning us in the woods. We had no other choice but to return to them after I disposed of the wicked woman. We brought them large, heavy pieces of her decadent, sugary home to prove our worth to them, which made our Papa seek the place out. From there, our sweets and pie business flourished within the candy house we only ever wanted to escape.

This damned candy house haunts me as I sleep within its walls, calling my name and taunting me. I started to hear her voice not too long ago, accusing me of murder.

Which is true. I am a murderer. I killed an old woman, but I had no choice. I had to protect my brother. I had to protect myself. I knew I would be her next feast once my brother was digesting in her bowels.

*"You are just as wicked as I,"* her voice whispers into my ears as I toss and turn in my bed. *"You are a vile, wicked little girl. You'll kill him one day. You need to if you never want to hear my voice again."*

I fight it every day. Mama has noticed how quiet I am but she rarely addresses it. If only I could tell her what I hear. If only I could tell her what I'm thinking. The madness taking control of my head, and the terrifying lack of control my hands battle against when they see Hansel standing too close to the fire.

But one night, it's too much. Her cracking voice hisses like a kettle in my head. It's too much, too much! I can't do this anymore. I go downstairs and find Hansel on a wooden stool, sitting alone by the fire sharpening a new knife for his field work. A small plate of mostly consumed cranberries, goat cheese, bread and toffee sit at his feet.

"Can't sleep, Gretel?" he asks as I approach him. He takes a moment to glance up and smile at me. "Me neither. I think it's all the sugar, it can't be good to consume this much of it."

He's so plump now. He's gained weight from eating in this damned house every day. I can't help but wonder if his blood tastes like cherries plucked straight from the tree, or figs drizzled with honey.

*"Do it, little girl,"* she whispers in my ear.

I step closer, too close before he realizes something is wrong.

*"I'll never leave you alone,"* she hisses. *"Go on, do it. Do it!"*

I can't explain myself as I raise both hands out, flat against his strong back.

*"Yes,"* she shrieks, her voice growling louder and louder. *"YES!"*

I can't even offer Hansel an apology as he tips forward, losing his balance and crashing face first into the dancing flames like I did to her.

She laughs wickedly, wildly in my head. And I keep wondering when she will go away. And then I realize as I stare into the fire with wide, horrified eyes …

*I am her now.*

It haunts me even more.

The End?

**Jessica L. Hughes** is an artist, writer and art educator living in Connecticut. She has been published in a small handful of independent art magazines, books and websites. She has written two novels and is awaiting their official publication. She plans to publish her book of poetry in the near future. You can keep up with her at www.agirlcalled672.com or follow her on Instagram: @agirlcalled672.

# Fairytale Endings and Other Disappointments

Adele Evershed

Their home was a shiny nugget; her husband christened it "Chestnut Cottage" and planted two chestnut trees as guards. His lettering was unsteady on the plaque he made to hang above the door, his fingers too unfamiliar with delicate tools to hold a brush with grace. He apologized for his clumsiness, but she told him she loved his hands; they were made for swinging a sledgehammer in his forge and scooping her up like a pearl. Then, he told her, "I'll teach our sons to play conkers, how to soak them in vinegar and bake them to make them hard."

She laughed and said, "What if we have daughters?"

He smiled and said, "Well, you can teach them to cook and sew and we will all live happily ever after here in the benevolent shadows of the spreading chestnut trees."

That first year she planted mint and cornflowers. When they flourished, she stitched them into a poppet. She had always done this secretly for women who came to her asking for a fertility charm, and it made her giddy to think she was finally doing it for herself. She placed a rose quartz inside–a stone of the heart. With each careful stitch, she imagined herself with child, then hid the poppet in a purse on her belt.

The first year the trees produced nuts, she harvested a bumper crop almost all worm-free. That winter, her belly swelled, and she put the poppet under her pillow. One warm day as she was picking Angelica for protection, her husband appeared with the poppet grasped in his fist.

"What is this witchery?" he stormed. "You promised me you had left your magic in your valley."

She tried to calm him, to explain it wasn't magic, it was women's wisdom.

His ears had been blocked long ago, so he took the poppet apart. Then he snarled, "If this was found, you would be put to death by the village. You are bringing great danger to our home."

After he stomped off, she crawled over and rescued the quartz, placing it in her belt, hoping it would still warm her unborn baby.

The following fall, the trees dropped plenty of husks, but they only had shriveled nuts inside, and when she gave birth, the midwife wrapped her babe in rags and spirited it away before she had time to say goodbye. That first time she hung her lullabies on a peg in the kitchen as a rebuke to her husband, but she also made sure they were close at hand for the next time she would need to sing.

Each time her belly grew, she whispered honeyed words trying to make the life within her stick, but there were to be no nut-brown boys, no sugar-spiced girls. After every miscarriage, she tore out another song. Soon all her music was gone. Her husband begged her to sing, feeling her silence like an itchy blanket he wanted to fling off. But she could not. Her music was suspended on hooks, and every time she reached for it while making soup or scrubbing floors, the black notes would beetle away and hide in the eves.

In her misery, she broke off pieces of herself, wanting her pain to be a material thing she could point to and say, "See, husband, see how I hurt."

Soon their bed was lumpy, as she had stuffed it with her hair. The windows were paned by tears, so they spun all that peered in or out. Her blinks gutted the candles, and her bitter words sat coiled as cushions. She placed them on all the chairs so her husband could not rest.

As time passed, her grief and his intolerance sucked them down to pips. The day he left, she took down the 'Chestnut Cottage' sign, not needing to be reminded of his hands. As she watched him pass the bare bones of the chestnut trees, she couldn't remember if they were to keep evil things at bay or to stop the bad things from leaving.

Returning to her kitchen, she noticed her songs had set like fossils into the wall. With an irritated flick of her hand, she changed them into swirly lollipops. Her muddy footprints became fondant mice squealing over the tiled floor, her spittle clotted to make batches of creamy fudge, and her empty paps sprayed sherbet dust on the walls, making them sparkle. Outside, the green paint of the cottage chipped away, leaving thick gingerbread underneath, and the roof split and re-thatched itself with cotton candy.

Later, when she felt at her loneliest, she burnt sugar, and the chimney puffed out welcoming marshmallow clouds, tempting children to come skipping through the wood with tales and curls, giggles, and grazed knees. Their lust for life satisfied her for a while. She fed them on bread made from crumbs of the moon and never let them out of her sight. But too soon, they complained that the bread was not filling or that they were sick of being swaddled, and they cried for their mothers. She only wanted them bright and happy, so as soon as she heard them wailing, she banished them with a sour belt. Yet she always took her moon bread to leave a luminescent breadcrumb trail for them to follow home. She hated the idea they might get lost forever in the wood.

Now in her kitchen, she rolls out the speckled dough, the air heavy with cinnamon, nutmeg, and longing. Cutting with care, she lifts the shape of a boy onto the baking tray. She sprinkles him with moon dust, unwrapping the quartz, she places it where his heart should be.

Taking down her music, she starts to hum, and soon she is singing the old songs again. Gretel whispers, "I will call you Hansel after my brother, but unlike him, you will never leave me."

She taps her feet as she waits for her gingerbread boy to cook. Then, taking him out of the oven, she holds him gently by his hands and dances around the kitchen and back again.

The End?

**Adele Evershed** was born in Wales. Her prose and poetry have been published in over a hundred journals and anthologies. She has been nominated for the Pushcart Prize and Best of the Net for poetry. Finishing Line Press is publishing Adele's first poetry chapbook, *Turbulence in Small Places* in 2023. Her Novella-in-Flash, *Wannabe*, was published by Alien Buddha Press in 2023.

# Check the Pulse

Kristen Whitney Daniels

"There are nights where I wake up drenched in sweat, as if I can still feel the heat licking my face. The fire consumes the oven, flames scorching my fingertips. I struggle to leave but she's holding my face to the blaze. I can't escape the smell of roasting flesh. And then the screaming starts, reverberating in my head. On a loop over and over and over."

"And how does that make you feel?"

*How does ... that ... make* me *feel?* I want to shout at him. How should my repeated nightmares from the cottage make me feel? Should I now feel hospitable to strangers? Adventurous? Grateful to be alive?

These last ten years have been a marathon to outmaneuver a past that always seems to know my next move. I fled those woods, never to look back, settling in a village where no one would know our names. I thought I could outrun it all but everything and nothing triggers a cascade of memories: locks on doors, smoke from a distant chimney, broken crumbs on the table.

A year ago, chatter about a new village psychotherapist made its way through the depths of the forest to my cottage. With few shreds of my sanity left, I took the dive into therapy thinking assistance would come in the form of meds–like cocaine–the "miracle drug" everyone raves about. Instead, I got fainting couches and open-ended questions doubting my feminine sensibilities. Somehow this cigar-obsessed therapist interpreted my trauma as a fantastical imagination from repressed childhood feelings.

Despite his ineptitude, I found catharsis in talking about those long-suppressed emotions, even if I couldn't safely share the whole truth of my tale. It was an opportunity to speak the version that will never make it into storybooks. The one that would never be whispered in warning to kids at bedtime. No, I somehow find myself on the side of Carthage versus Rome, General Cornwallis in Yorktown, and Napoleon in Russia. On the side of the losers, the defeated and conquered. As history has repeatedly shown, the past is only kind to the victors.

I was in my late thirties when I found two emaciated children nibbling on a wooden shutter of my cottage as if it was candy. As I tried to take in the strange scene before me, the boy–without a shred of pretense–blurted out *"what an ugly, very, very old witch."* As an unmarried woman without children, I was used to witchcraft accusations by villagers. I also knew my advanced arthritis and the milky lens from cataracts didn't help quell the rumors. And yet those words still struck their mark.

Despite the crude assessment, I couldn't leave these malnourished, hallucinating children on their own. I welcomed them, fed them, and clothed them. In return, the children concocted a story that I was a witch, hellbent on kidnapping and devouring them.

Why would I want to lure more mouths to feed in a famine? I failed to understand how the children's history of neglect bred a toxic desire to prove their worthiness. Those children would do anything to earn their father's acceptance, even at my expense. Even kick a blind woman face first into a scalding oven. Fortunately for me, their desire to be the hero in their own story made them hasty. They forgot the cardinal rule of vanquishing any foe: check the pulse. One must be unequivocally certain that when you say someone is dead, they are positively dead.

I felt powerless long before those children ransacked my cottage. I am a physically disabled, single, middle-aged, non-conventionally attractive blind woman. I knew what it was to be abandoned to the periphery, whispers of disgust trailing my every move. But now I was left disfigured from scalp to breast, pushing me into social pariah status. And those wandering, discarded, starving children? Robbed me of every bauble and heirloom. Living off my wealth while I sit here miserable, in therapy, pondering how to let go of a past that was never finished with me.

"Hexia." The therapist's voice drew me from my thoughts. "You've been here for a year and we've made no progress. What do you seek from your sessions? Closure? Forgiveness?"

"Closure?" I laughed sardonically. There is no such thing as closure when your scars speak on your behalf, when every stranger is a threat, and every act of kindness is a ploy. How does one move on from a marred life?

"You ought to find resilience, let go of the hysteria," he continued. "Take those new villagers in town, the brother and sister. You must've heard the terrible ordeal they went through as children. They're settling in so nicely, writing books. They share their tale of torture, while overcoming it to save the townsfolks. What a resilient pair."

I can excuse their hunger for food, stability, and family. But profiting off their deceit while I live in squalor? I expect panic or fear to course through my veins at the mention of their names. Instead, an icy calmness descends. A clear vision of reparations. Perhaps fate does intervene, I think to myself.

At home after the session, I look at myself in the mirror for the first time in years: my face resembling the side of a melted candle. Droopy, worn, and bubbled. Why is it that heroes never have to atone for their wrongdoings? Why would they when they're convinced of their own convictions? But now, as a plan starts brewing from within, I am filled with hope, purpose, and meaning.

Surely, destiny interceded to devise this fortuitous encounter between us all. After all this time, fate's little breadcrumbs bringing back our diverged paths.

I know I will forever be the villain in this story. It is impossible to undo what has already been fabricated. Society will always find a way to recast women as witches. But like Heavens' avenging angels, I might as well find out if vengeance can beget forgiveness.

The End?

**Kristen Whitney Daniels** is proud to finally call herself a fiction writer. Kristen works as the assistant director of a national nonprofit and previously worked as an award-winning journalist and a case manager. In addition to her work, she is a disability advocate, fighting to make #insulin4all a reality. In her free time, she loves reading, embroidering, outdoor movie nights, and being an auntie.

# The Steve Summers Show Season 3, Episode 12

Andrea J. Rockower

*(Raucous Steve Summers Show theme music.)*

## Steve

Hi, friends, and welcome to the Steve Summers Show, where no matter what the season, it's always hot, hot, hot right here in our studio! Today we are going to journey to the unpredictable land of fairy tales and meet the people who actually had the Grimm experiences–and I do mean "grim"–to see if there really is such a thing as living "happily ever after." My first guest is–well–let's call him "Harry."

*(Corny bridge music while Harry, a man in his 30s, drags himself on stage and sits.)*

So, tell me, what is it like being you, Hansel–oops, or should I say Harry–and where has life taken you these past years?

## Harry

Instead of a fairytale, my life has been a nightmare! Psychologists have had a field day with me and my family–you know, the whole abandonment thing. But do you know what it really feels like to be Hansel? Even my very name sounds funny to some of you, doesn't it? Sure, I was that cute little German boy in the illustration with freckles, wearing shorts and suspenders and it all seemed so sweet and charming. But what if YOU were the one who had lived it?

My mother died when I was little, my father was weak and left me alone in a forest with my poor little sister who has since moved away and hasn't talked to me for almost ten years–and I'm talking storybook years! Even she was forced to change her name.

There's nothing "cute" about being a starving child abandoned in a forest with hungry wolves around. And in case you've forgotten, in the world of my childhood, hungry wolves were always waiting in dark forests for innocent little children to come along.

Maybe some of you even sat through Humperdinck's opera about my sister and me. That exploiter should have paid us royalties! And do you know what the final insult was? Hansel is a "trouser role." It's played by a female mezzo-soprano! Well, excuse me for living!

It's been tough. Once colleagues find out my real identity, they keep teasing me. They say things like: "When are you coming to work in your lederhosen, Harry?" or "Look out, you're getting crumbs on the floor" or even "That supervisor is a real witch, isn't she, Harry?" My last few jobs were in the food industry. I was an assembly-line taste-tester for Sunshine Cookies, the only job I seemed qualified for, but they accused me of over-sampling the marshmallow creams and I got fired.

Well, I think it is now time for me to turn the page on this story. I'm thinking seriously about buying the acreage where the woods are and turning it into a Hansel and Gretel theme park called "Gingerbread Land" with a roller coaster ride through a huge oven. Steve, maybe you could help me promote it.

### Steve

Let's hold that thought and right now, reunite you with your sister, Gigi, whom you haven't seen or spoken to in ten years.

*(Segue music and applause as Gigi enters the stage and sits.)*

So, Gretel … I mean Gigi … how do you feel about what your brother has said?

### Gigi

Yes, I do feel bad about what's happened to my brother, but it hasn't been easy for me either. The only way I could survive was by putting as much distance as I could between me and the past. If you think it hasn't left any scars, you're crazy. Being so hungry as a child and then coming upon a cottage made of cookies and gingerbread and eating my fill led me to a life of bulimia. Yes, I'm the queen of splurge and purge. And no amount of therapy is helping.

Okay, so I was the one who gave the witch the final "push" into the oven. Well, it was a case of roast or be roasted! But it was not a crime. I challenge you all to check the penal codes of any civilized country. See if you can find a law against a child pushing a fairytale witch into an oven. Why, in some countries, I'd be considered a saint!

Oh, Steve, it has been hard for me, too, to settle down in a job or a relationship. I keep looking for strong men, but always seem to hook up with weak ones, just like my father. And I stay far away from forests. I'm "dendrophobic." Too many trees and I just freak out. I'm a mess!

## Steve

Terrible … just terrible. Audience, what do you think?

*(Audience applauds.)*

Maybe I can offer some solace to you both with our next surprise guest. Madam, won't you please join us?

*(Mysterious music. A woman in a dark black veil enters and takes a seat.)*

## Woman

It's okay, children. You needn't worry. Really. It is true, I *was* the woman in the cottage in the forest. Yes, my house *was* made of cookies and gingerbread. But I have been unfairly portrayed by the Grimms as a kind of child molester. I am actually a Wiccan woman and *adore* children. I think there must have been some kind of miscommunication between us those many years ago. When I said you both were so cute I could just "eat you up," I didn't mean it literally. It was just a bit of teasing. I certainly *do not* eat human flesh. I was just lonely and wanted to keep the two of you as my sweet little pets. Once you threw me into the oven, Gretel dear, my body was covered in burns. I shall live with the infamy of that day and will for centuries to come.

*(The Steve Summers Show theme music is played.)*

## Steve

Well, I'm afraid that's all we have time for today. Happy endings? I don't think so! More like a bunch of whackos! Anyway, please join me tomorrow when we will meet with some celebrity impersonators who have served jail time for stalking their idols and have no plans to stop.

*(Audience applause.)*

The End!

Since retiring from her position at a university performing arts center, **Andrea J. Rockower** has been busy studying and writing plays and short stories and trying to improve her skills in French. So far, she hasn't dared to combine the two endeavors.

# Stories and Authors

The stories collected in **Whatever Happened to Hansel and Gretel?** were written by participants in Kim Kovach's spring 2023 fiction writing classes offered via Zoom through the Pound Ridge Library in New York and the Trumbull Library in Connecticut. Permission for printing these stories has been granted by the authors.

*Hansel and Gretel's Cautionary Tale* by Angela Blake Fields

*Sweet Magic* by Claudia Wolen

*Hansel and Gretel Plus Ten* by Richard Mendes

*Gretel's Regret* by Kim Kovach

*A Tale Within A Tale* by Martha Paszek

*The Gingerbread Forest* by Janet M. Bair

*Beyond the Gingerbread House* by Janice Boland

*Hans and Greta* by Patricia Humphreys

*Gretel's Revenge* by Lisa Acerbo

*ZauberDorf* by Claire Quinn

*The Further Adventures of Hansel and Gretel* by Everett W. Fields

*Hansel and Gretel–A Journey to Freedom* by Virginia Bulzacchelli

*Ever After* by Kelly Gavin Guerra

*Ten Years After* by John-Paul Marciano

*Hansel and Gretel, Ten Years After* by Martha Jankovic

*Hansel and Gretel* by Carmella Cammarota

*Hansel and Gretel, Redux* by Debbie Gilbert

*All That Glitters* by Constance Taylor

*Hansel and Gretel: The Aftermath* by Jennie Scalisi

*Hans and Greta–The "Lebensfreude"* by Shari Kay Mokhtari

*The Final Ingredient* by Jessica L. Hughes

*Fairytale Endings and Other Disappointments* by Adele Evershed

*Check the Pulse* by Kristen Whitney Daniels

*The Steve Summers Show, Season 3, Episode 12* by Andrea J. Rockower